My Way or the Hemming

"The Soulful Passage of Tommy Typical"

*To Michael —
(BLONE)
[signature]
8/04*

Copyright © 2006 Tom Hicks

10-Digit ISBN 1-59113-974-0
13-Digit ISBN 978-1-59113-974-4

All rights reserved. No part of this publication may be reproduced, stored in a retrieval system, or transmitted in any form or by any means, electronic, mechanical, recording or otherwise, without the prior written permission of the author.

Printed in the United States of America.

Booklocker.com, Inc.
2006

My Way or the Hemingway

"The Soulful Passage of Tommy Typical"

Tom Hicks

Aloha

I am both a man born of reason living in a material world and a man born of spirit living in a mystical world. God's beautiful irony has led me not to confliction, but instead to endless and magical possibilities in this life and through my imagination in the one to come. I would like to especially thank Don Olea for his creativity in converting my thoughts to enchanting images.

Tommy "Hickey" Typical

What we call life is a journey to death.
What we call death is the gateway to life.
Uncle "Anonymous" Typical

"The Soulful Passage of Tommy Typical"

My Own Fishy Demise

"Many men fish all of their lives without realizing that it's not the fish they are after." Henry David Thoreau

Trout, as is their God-given nature, can act in mystifying ways and anyone who has tried to catch one knows it full well. The rare Brook Trout, known affectionately as "specs" by the locals, reside in the upper elevations. Brown Trout thrive in warmer, lower environments. And finally due to mass stocking, the non-native and colorful Rainbow Trout are quite plentiful. The three species of my favorite fish can be found in the streams nearby or within a reasonable drive from my hometown in East Tennessee. Some in larger numbers than others just like people. The world of people and fish keeps changing.

As an inexperienced boy, I lived a fairly short distance from the regal Great Smokies. The native Cherokee called the misty mountains the "place of the blue smoke". Those foothills, I figure, were called "great" because they were so ascetically majestic. Throughout all of the surrounding counties, including Anderson County where I lived, the streaming waters sustained the hallowed fish I came to pursue in my youth. But like Little Jackie Paper, who lost his magical dragon, Puff, for a season, I too temporarily lost my childhood and my innocent pursuit of Mr. Trout, the mysterious one who got away. Like all things, that, too comes full circle. And as they say, "Once a fisherman, always a fisherman," and I don't know who *they* are, but *they* do seem to know. Don't *they*?

For you see, the Lord too, as is His Divine prerogative, also works in mysterious ways. To proof my point, I have chosen to tell you about the most bamboozling ways from my own limited perspective right here in the detail of my stories that I know will sound a little odd but as Papa Hemingway used to say and still does I reckon, "My aim is to put down on paper what I see and what I feel in the best and simplest way." Fish tales and human tales are simultaneously fictitious and factual.

Now that doesn't mean that it's not a little tricky to explain from a human point of view for the weirdest series of fishy events recently occurred to me. Frankly I'm not sure how I'm even in this uncertain position to write about it, but apparently I am, so here goes lest my opportunity gets away and if you fish you know how quickly that can happen. I remember the first stringer of fish I took home and how quickly the flapping stopped after I removed them from their life source, the precious water. I wondered where their energy went. I was still wondering that same thing forty years later until I had this dream one summer night, a premonition of what would someday unfold.

While I lay sleeping, my time it seemed had officially come. I had kicked the old minnow bucket. It's a regrettable moment from a mortal perspective that we all know is approaching but usually choose to place somewhere in the back of our minds as we obliviously deal with the hubbub of life on earth. I'm almost convinced that it is a methodology that keeps us functional in this realm of perceived mortality. Admittedly, I was somewhat taken aback when I discovered that it was unfortunately my turn at bat and I arrived at the symbolic Pearly Gates that turned out to be quite real after all. Reality, it seems, is a tricky thing, like hooking the aforementioned crafty trout.

I was right on schedule, I do believe, a rarity for me. So, I wasn't late for my own funeral as I was told repeatedly by others for many years that I most certainly would be. The joke was on them. But I was here nonetheless at that appointed place we all long for and fear simultaneously and in that regard the joke was on me. As is usually the case, it all balances out in the long run. That's something I learned in my life and times and on my trips to Las Vegas. The circumstances surrounding my big event are a tad unclear. Life can be like that when the pace gets frantic and circumstances seem a bit out of the ordinary. It's a little like the murk that gets stirred up when you disturb the bottom of a clear stream.

In fact, the very last thing I truly remember was going to sleep in a comfortable room in the tower at the Ramada Inn near O'Hare Airport after consuming a *Steak Diane* of momentous dimensions and a goodly portion of a bottle of red wine, a Merlot I believe, that was so tasty I tipped the wine steward twenty extra bucks even though the wine was already overpriced and just perhaps, no definitely, I was under the dreamy influence of the juice. I knew the chap was on a commission and I felt generous in it's a business deduction anyway frame of mind. Timing is a big part of making money. At least it had been for me up until that point in time. Unfortunately, now what would all the money in the world get me? Jesus, as usual, was 100% correct when he said that your soul had more value than all those worldly goods anyhow. In the end, if I may get a tad philosophical, just what was the big deal about making deals? That shook my capitalist timbers.

Not to be cliché, but that's not the conclusion of my memorable "last meal". I knew I shouldn't have had dessert last night, but the table side preparation of my favorite dessert medley, cherries jubilee, peach flambé, and bananas foster that I had previously nicknamed *Suicide*, how apropos, caused me to exceed even the bounds of my own gastronomic limitations, a record that I had previously recorded at some other fine eating establishment in Chicagoland. It was always a glorious way to complete a good meal.

There at the Cafe La Cave, on 2777 Mannheim Rd., in Des Plaines, Illinois, *Continental Cuisine* is served by courteous smartly dressed waiters and my meal like always was exquisite and it proved to be the meal of a lifetime, mine anyways. I usually became hungry thinking about good meals, but here where I now found myself I wasn't the least bit ravenous. I had heard that might be the case. I found that I liked being hungry because like any clear cut problem, there was a logical solution. Just feed yourself and the problem is solved. That's how I got my limits of trout. I knew they were hungry so I solved their problem by providing a solution to their problem and at the same time as an angler I solved mine. It was a win-win situation especially since I was a catch and release fisherman. Until now, I had not fully considered the pain inflicted by the hook.

At any rate sometime during the night as I lay in the king size bed of my spacious hotel room, I transcended the earthly experience and headed for my heavenly reward. I don't really know what happened but I was granted my wish of dying in my sleep. I'm thinking it was probably an old fashioned heart attack. It was exactly the way I had wished to go, in my sleep. Now I wished I hadn't made that wish even jokingly. Still I wondered if during the big event I made a noise and if like the tree that falls in the woods, if no one heard it did I really make a sound. Would I ever know the answer? *"Pshaw!"* Grandma would say, *"You need to spend your time worrying about something that matters."* To which I would now reply, "It matters to me." Though for the life of me I didn't know why at that exact moment.

Back to my recent unplanned, at least by me, journey, it was a short trip, time wise, as far as I could determine. Distance wise I had no clue how far I'd traveled, though I was convinced that it was more than a few light years since no scientist had ever set eyes on Heaven with a capital "H" even with the Hubble telescope. Unlike what I had seen in the movies and read in books, the Good Book, excepted, and accepted of course.

Yeah gang, I knew exactly where I was and I didn't have to ask anyone if I was dead or what was up. I understood in blunt earthly terms I was now *deceased,* though the word did not adequately describe this situation at all. Hence, I will use some popular terms and images that you might understand better. You know the current Westernized images that have been widely employed for Heaven, but don't for a New York minute confuse the idealism of pop culture with this ultimate reality. Though there are a few similarities, the reality of the situation is as far apart from the perception as the East is from the West. So with the clear understanding that I shall use these familiar representations just to set the stage so to speak concerning unfamiliar and awe-inspiring individuals and places, I shall cautiously proceed on this journey of my soul. But it was one that billions had trod before me in their own unique way.

I suddenly found myself in the presence of a large man whom I believed to be St. Peter, the very one I was expecting according to what I was told as a kid and whom I somehow instinctively knew upon sight. Okay so I may have made a connection with the heavenly backdrop. While utterly inexplicable it strangely seemed logical to me. He appeared younger than I had ever imagined him to be and he spoke my native tongue impeccably though it was apparent he wasn't from the South. My guess would have been that the accent was Midwestern perhaps Ohio or maybe Indiana. That inflection had a calming All-American effect of comfort to me.

"The Soulful Passage of Tommy Typical"

The Pearly Gates was not what I would call a traditional gateway. I had expected something almost grandiose, but a small wooded path beside what I recognized immediately as a trout stream with huge potential. I had an innate sense about such things. The pathway disappeared into a dense forest that was greener than any patch of woods I had ever seen. The shallow clear creek had plenty of strategically placed flat and ridged stones to create the perfect little riffles beyond the deep pools where big old hungry trout were prone to relax and work up their appetites. As Peter Parker would say, "My spider senses were tingling." I almost said a dirty word but caught myself prior to the faux pas.

The setting looked vaguely familiar and extremely promising from an angler's perspective. While I inspected it admiringly, my greeter told me that the entry appeared differently to each person. As *mi amigo* explained this to me, he cited that first impressions were important here. I was quite impressed by my first impression and told him so. He graciously said he would pass the praise along. I had no doubt that he would. Scoring brownie points here couldn't hurt one's case. I was still trying to work the crowd as my business partner would say.

I asked the obvious questions about loved ones and friends who had gone before me and the old saint assured me they were waiting patiently along with the Big Guy who was preparing my coming out party. That revelation elated me and in fact I felt I had never been so happy in all my life. It was sort of like my first skydiving experience. For the moment nothing seemed to matter but getting through this experience successfully. Then actuality set in yet again and I asked about my family that I had left behind. *Were they okay? Would they be well cared for? Could I see them from here?* Questions like that swelled up from the depths of my former self or my new self or both. I didn't know. I couldn't distinguish.

Peter touched me on the arm and said the living would get along fine without me and that response and the way he said it both soothed me and I'll have to admit troubled me because as hard as I tried I still had feelings that I was indispensable to those left behind. Apparently I wasn't. That old saying that everyone is replaceable popped into my mind. Peter read my thoughts and told me that while I would be sorely missed I wasn't indispensable at all. "In fact," he started to say something more and then caught himself and stopped putting a finger to his lips. I finished the sentence in my head..."The world would keep on spinning. The show must go on."

My elation was squelched temporarily and that led to a new nonstop barrage of deep questions. The age old *whys and hows*. I didn't even allow my ethereal friend time to reply before I reeled off another question that I felt I had to have the answer to and eventually the patient Peter raised his hand as a gesture of cessation and said calmly, "There'll be plenty of time for that. Right now I want to give you a gift."

"A gift! I exclaimed in disbelief as my mood turned cheerful again. "Just being here is a gift." It sounded so trite. What was wrong with me? Was I trying to score brownie points again? My wife had always told me I was a big ham. As usual she was right. But I was excited. Would it be wrapped in pretty paper?

Old St. Pete didn't notice or if he did, he didn't let on. Instead he said, "Well, the Boss insists on it. Since humans all live at different times in different places, He thought it would be nice if you and everyone else who shows up here could spend a little time, a two week holiday, with someone that you admired or were simply interested in while you lived on Earth. Then after that we link up with some old friends for a little more fishing before you move on. Tommy, we get all kinds of requests. So don't be shy or feel that you have to hold back. Go for it as you say. The only guideline is that the person is departed like you and not a close relative since most of your time will be spent with your family for the next couple of centuries."

"You're kidding," I retorted before I thought about whether kidding or humor of any kind was allowed here. Anyway knowing that a future family reunion was in the mix, I felt better. I had a lot to say to my bloodline.

"No, not about this," Peter responded unperturbedly interrupting my rambling, "What *do* you think?"

"The Soulful Passage of Tommy Typical"

I sat down on a tuft of soft grass, the kind I had used as a kid for chewing on as I watched and named white puffy clouds. I took my sweet time and he waited good-naturedly. In fact he sat down too and hummed softly. I believe it was an old hymn I recognized from my childhood, one my grandpa hummed but I couldn't name at that moment. I thought extensively about my dreams and aspirations and what it was I truly wanted right now.

Have you ever noticed that when you try to focus on something big, it's at that exact instant that little bizarre things creep in? It's at those times you might laugh nervously for some unknown reason. I thought that aspect of my nature would change when I was made *perfect*. It hadn't, but I'll have to admit that here, in this place, priorities were different and I couldn't yet fully explain how, but I knew I was inexplicably changed, to boot, in some fundamental way and yet I felt wholly in tact. That was never what I expected but it felt so natural.

My Way or the Hemingway

Key West Overture

"Fishing not a matter of life and death - it's much more important than that!" *Anonymous*

I walked guardedly over to the water's edge and looked in. With a lifelong awareness that fish are wary, to my surprise there he was the same Trout that I had first seen as a boy and had chased incessantly for the rest of my life. I squinted, a trait I had picked up in middle age as a means to focus my aging eyes and peered intently at the clear water. Now more than the water was clear. Of all the important things I had forgotten in my lifetime, this recall was as real as the day it occurred. I was six and one half back then going on seven. Half years mattered in those days. The time between birthdays seemed like an eternity. I laughed because no one on earth really had a clue what eternity was like.

"I want to spend my holiday with Hemingway," I declared after an ample musing period. "Is that acceptable?" I had opened my eyes widely with hands extended palms up. I nodded at St. Peter as I leaned forward, and repeated my application in what I hoped was a convincing manner, "Okay?" I asked as I touched his hand. He smiled and laughingly agreed and I looked around just in time to see Mr. Trout do a one eighty in the stream and disappear in the riffles. Apparently everyone was on board for this ride. But it had been a tough decision between Gene Autry and Hemingway. One Christmas I had gotten a Gene Autry cowboy outfit including a six-shooter and a big soft teddy bear named Hemingway who shared my bed with me. That was a great holiday and little did I know at the time that I would have to make the choice between the two on another holiday.

Regardless, an instant later, I found myself sitting at a bar. It seemed a little familiar but I had frequented more than my share of drinking establishments in my lifetime. I was of Irish descent. I was quite sure that I hadn't been in this particular one but most dark bars looked and smelled alike. The joint was really crowded and very loud in a good way. I was in need of getting my bearings, the compass in my head set straight, as my ex brother-in-law always said. So I fought my way through the mass of living, breathing, smelly humanity and stepped outside in the middle of one of those evening humidity driven thundershowers, the kind that get you wet even if you are under a shelter. I looked up at a hanging sign just to see where in the world I was. It was a simple marker that blew back and forth in the warm wind and plainly read *Sloppy Joe's Bar.* I wiped my eyes and looked again. There was no mistaking that this was exactly where I was if one is after one once was. Damn confusing.

"No way," I kept saying in disbelief to myself knowing that something magical had and was in the midst of happening.

"Yes way," a smiling vagrant who was standing beside me responded. "Got a buck?" He asked. The man looked familiar but his face was hard to see since he had a baseball hat that sported a Marlins logo pulled down over his eyes and as I fumbled through my pockets looking for money, he laughed and said, "Never mind, big spender. I was just testing your charity." He began walking away. Then over his shoulder from the distance, I could hear St. Peter's voice faintly say again, "Absolutely yes way." I always thought that I was being tested when I was given an opportunity to help someone. Now I knew for sure. After I closed my eyes and shook my head violently for a moment to see if I could wake up from this madness, I looked up and he was gone. "You got me, Peter!" I shouted. Apparently he was a shape shifter. This was a weird trip I was on and time and space were out of kilter around these parts. But given I had died earlier, I was more than willing to play since it was the only game in town and one I just remembered that I had chosen. Free will is quite complicated.

So I stood there wet from rain and perspiration for a while knowing I couldn't figure this out on my own. The shower stopped and within minutes it was hot and humid with steam rising from the pavement. I could smell the salty ocean nearby as well as the aroma of something good that was cooking and I remembered how much I loved to smell things. In fact, many of my fondest memories were smells of familiar places and people. I particularly liked the smell of soap. I thought about many things in a short period of time as people walked hurriedly by me. Finally, just to prove I wasn't the one who was an apparition, I approached another passerby, a smiling guy wearing a bright yellow tee shirt from Jimmy Buffett's place, *Margaritaville*, wearing a pair of frayed baggy shorts; and worn FloJos, who had asked me "Are you okay, dude?"

"Where am I, Pal?" I asked needing more confirmation.

Without delay, he said glibly shaking his finger vigorously as he rattled on, "Hey man, you, my bud, are on the on the corner of Greene and Duval Streets in sunny when it's daytime, downtown, Key West, Florida, dude."

I smiled and said "Thanks," then gave my informant a shaky thumbs up signal as he strolled away speaking into the night air, "Anytime, Brah. Anytime."

I could tell you some things about time, dude, I thought.

Alright. Here was the story as far as I knew. I wa*s* really here, whatever *real* happened to mean now. So I did what my old football coach instructed me to do during my short career on the grid iron. I took the ball and ran with it and waited for someone to knock the living daylights out of me.

I walked back in and took my seat again, allowing my eyes to adjust to the abrupt change from intense outdoor light to the dimness of the dark bar. It's a shadow world when you do that for the first few seconds and then things start to clear up a bit. I could hear a combination of steel drum music and pool sticks striking cue balls. Sitting next to me was a man I immediately recognized, from the hundreds of photographs I had perused in my life. It was Mr. Ernest Hemingway. Here he sat in the flesh or something that closely resembled flesh. He was casually sipping on a drink. Well, he wasn't actually sipping. It was more like a controlled gulp. As I watched him enjoy his libation, I knew that an old trout was partly responsible for my decision. Right now I didn't know whether to thank him or not, the jury was out.

While I continued to gape in total incredulity, a handsome giant of a black man, the bartender that looked as big as I remember Refrigerator Perry being from his NFL days asked me, "What'll you have my friend?" I looked at Hemingway's glass and said authoritatively, "Whatever he's drinking. That's my poison."

"Well, sir, he's drinking mojitos tonight because he told me he was expecting someone and that's what that someone would want, Papa's signature drink. You are that someone, right?"

"Yes sir I guess I am," I acknowledged. I decided a long time ago to be respectful to everyone not knowing just whom you might be speaking to and if they were armed. I chose to be especially kind if they were bigger than the side of a mountain.

"And Mr. Hemingway is the host for your holiday," he added and winked. Apparently he was in on this whole affair.

"I believe so." I verified licking my dry lips. He observed my gesture of thirstiness with a bartender's eye for the likes of a man who needs a drink to quench his thirst and calm his nerves.

"Then a mojito it is, partner." He turned and began preparing my cocktail with an assurance that it would be made perfectly. It was indeed.

I couldn't believe it. I knew intuitively who he was. I was talking to the Kahuna himself, the legendary bartender, "Big Skinner" in the flesh. There on the wall behind the bar in its rightful place of honor was the 119-pound sailfish caught by Hemingway. Unlike my trout, he hadn't' gotten away. Trophies can be tangible or figurative.

"Dang," I whispered to myself revealing my redneck roots. I was thoroughly overwhelmed at the sight of that big fish hanging there.

It was an impressive trophy from an era when such things were de rigueur. I looked around for more prizes. The bar was enormous and as I scanned the room, there were the well-known paintings of boxers, men of pugilistic renown that decorated the walls. I took a deep sustained breath and the smell of cigar smoke permeated my lungs. This place was not politically correct. The building had the look of Old Havana; you know what I mean, tiled floors and ceiling fans that swirled endlessly. I was later told by an old drunk that Joe Russell, the salty proprietor had paid a whopping $2,500 for this place after moving from across the street.

While I was spending copious amounts of time just rubber necking the joint, Big Skinner returned and set my drink in front of me. I was plenty thirsty. I knew that this carefully prepared concoction was generally favored when Hemingway was in Cuba but I just couldn't wait to set the mood. I wanted to have a belt with him right now. I slurped it down reminiscing that it tasted similar to the mint juleps served at the Kentucky Derby. I had attended the Derby once with a fellow from New York State.

The mojito, a blend of rum, fresh mint, sugar, lemon juice, and water served over ice hit the spot and since I needed a little time to finish thinking about old Wild Bill from the Empire State and some more of his exploits, I promptly ordered up another drink subconsciously trying to muster up enough courage to talk to Papa, a thrill that few from my generation had experienced.

I eventually turned on the squeaky bar stool and cleared my nervous throat before talking. "So howzit going?" He took another generous snort from his glass and grinned broadly staring straight ahead. I was more than a little intimidated by him. Time, even though it didn't exist in a normal state here, froze for a spell like the ice cubes in his drink. I relished that indefinable moment.

I remembered seeing a photograph once of him circa 1940, shortly after he returned from Europe and in that picture, he looked just like he did now. His hair was dark and thick and tousled by the wind. His dense mustache accented his large forehead. There were strategic wrinkles and age lines that creased the interesting beefy face. While I was studying his unforgettable features as discretely as I could, he had placed his glass on the bar and crossed his tanned arms and his barrel chest was fully exposed since the blue work shirt was unbuttoned. His brow was damp and like any sportsman of his era smelled of fish and booze. I couldn't have been more pleased. He was exactly as I anticipated he would be and when he began speaking, he sounded just like I had always imagined he would.

"I thought we would spend the evening here getting to know each other and then you can bunk with me tonight. If we make it home. Regardless, tomorrow we fish."

"Sure, I agreed. By the way, I'm Tom Hicks. I go by Tommy Typical. " I thought about extending my hand but his arms remained crossed and I didn't.

"I know," he smiled again and went back to his drink. So much for the formalities. He did not seem to be interested in prolonging the introductions beyond the fact that he decided to call me Hickey. I was okay with that moniker. I had been called that name as a kid. In fact I was "Little Hickey". My dad was "Big Hickey". Yeah, Hickey was alright. It made me feel young again in a way and it was okay with Papa. That mattered most.

He told me that Key West is where he earned that nickname "Papa" amid his fishing friends known as "The Key West Mob". He told me I could call him Papa, too. I was delighted at that invitation. Nicknames are about familiarity and bragging. He explained that since we would be crossing time lines, there was no need to change names as we enjoyed the holiday. "It could get confusing," he added, "to be all the names that you acquire in a lifetime. Like *son of a bitch* for example. I've been called that a few times. Probably earned the title."

At that instant, someone yelled from across the room. "Hemingway, why did the chicken cross the road?"

He nudged me and grinned, then yelled out, "To die. In the rain. Alone."

I waited and there was silence for a few seconds and then a roar of laughter filled the saloon. I joined in. I was having a very good time so far with the old self proclaimed SOB. I wondered if I could be Little SOB.

After we chatted for a little while longer, he began working the room stopping here and there to jaw. A few minutes later, I recalled how much Papa loved Key West as I watched him shooting a game of pool in the rear area of the bar with a tall lean man, a dangerous looking chap. There were several large pool tables situated there and farther back were tables where various games of chance were being played. He liked it here because it must have been like living in a foreign country while remaining in America. He liked playing both sides against the middle and once remarked about his affection for this place, "It's the best place I've ever been anytime, anywhere, flowers, tamarind trees, guava trees, coconut palms...Got tight last night on absinthe and did knife tricks."

I was working on my fourth mojito, having slowed down after twelve bells, but the rowdy crowd was still sizable though it had been reduced somewhat as the evening hours had advanced and the reasonable ones considered how they would feel in the morning. The noise level had remained the same. I had lingered around the bar talking with Big Skinner who told me that Hemingway was getting married in two weeks giving me a shrug when I asked how time really worked here. All he knew was that Papa met his bride to be, Martha Gellhorn, here in Key West. She was a writer and they clicked and then they played hanky panky for four years before all hell broke loose at home and around the world. Combat comes in all flavors he said.

"It all started over that war in Spain," my new friend said. "Pauline, his second wife sided with Franco because he was for the Catholics. Papa backed the communists because they supported the government the people had voted in. He traveled with Martha and they fell in love. War does that you know. Danger and romance go hand in hand.

But they also fought for the good news stories. He likes his women feisty like that. Well, it would have been a perfect love story except Papa was already married. They met right here at Sloppy Joe's around Christmas time in 1936. Papa was sure right about Franco. He ain't nothing but a dictator like Hitler and Mussolini. The world didn't need another one Papa says."

By three a.m., I was both a little tired and a whole lot drunk, and had switched to the drink that was purportedly invented by Hemingway himself. The "Papa Doble" or the Hemingway daiquiri. Rumor has it that Hemingway invented the drink here at Sloppy Joe's. Some sources say the drink had been around since the turn of the century. Regardless it was flavorsome and potent. After you had a few, you felt very impotent. It consisted of two ounces of white or light rum, the juice from two limes, the juice from half a grapefruit, and Maraschino liqueur floating on the top, served over crushed ice. Ice of any kind must have been a luxury here in the early years. Now it's a necessity.

My hat's off to Big Skinner for watering them down a bit and keeping me afloat as I was fading fast, but Hemingway was still going strong, and was now flipping knives around like a juggler with a small group of interesting men that I couldn't even begin to describe but knew were as fascinating as their ringleader.

I laughed thinking that some of them might be such legends as John Dos Passos, Waldo Pierce, J.B. Sullivan, Hamilton Adams, Captain Eddie Saunders, and Henry Strater. Not everybody looks like their pictures. Those men were just a few of the group of modern day philosophers who gathered on this spot regularly and created this unforgettable myth, though it's highly unlikely they knew they were doing anything other than having a good time.

I believe that it was Dos Passos who once told Hemingway and Pauline about Key West in the first place. After leaving Paris, the couple decided to stop here on their way home. It's funny how that works in our lives. Anyway, thanks to Uncle Gus, Pauline's relative, they bought the now cat ridden house at 907 Whitehead Street and the rest is the stuff that folklore is made of and we all love stories sprinkled with stardust. Joni Mitchell wrote of my Woodstock Generation that "We are stardust, we are golden, and we got to get ourselves back to the garden."

I decided that I would lay my head down on the bar for a minute or two just to rest my eyes. I couldn't keep up with this crowd. The next thing I knew I felt someone shaking me vigorously and I on impulse looked at my watch made of solid aluminum. My trusty timepiece has an eerie moon glow electroluminescent dial light that let's you see the time, in all conditions. A fly fisher casting to a big trout is etched on the back of the watch in stainless steel. My chronometer was good to 3 ATM (100 feet) and totally water resistance. It had a thermometer on the back and an integrated hook sharpener not to mention attached nippers and an LED flashlight and compass. I liked having information at my fingertips. I bought it for a hundred bucks when a hundred bucks meant a lot to me and it had been worth every penny.

It was five-thirty. Papa stood beside me holding a small cup he called a tacita, not too much larger than a thimble. "It's café cubano and you don't sip it, sport. You throw it down like a shot of liquor. Café cubano is a strong potion usually about double the strength of American coffee. Big Skinner brews it on a stove in the back and mine is much stronger than most. C'mon now, bottoms up. It'll clear out the cobwebs."

I choked it down and found that it wasn't really all that bad. It just took some getting used to and within fifteen minutes, I was revived as I felt the caffeine surging through my veins. We switched to a steaming cup of Café con Leche, which is Cuban coffee with milk, and as we sipped Papa said, "Let's take a walk. I wish to show you something special."

We stepped outside and walked a short distance stopping briefly to watch the sunrise. The colors exploded in orange and red and the brightness surrounded us and wrapped itself around us. It was going to be a warm sunny day in South Florida. Sunrises are always original.

"We are going to Havana after we fish. We have only two weeks together and we won't be back here again. There's a lot to do, Hickey." He must have caught the play on words because he repeated it, "do-hickey, ha!"

"That's fine with me. After what I've seen recently, I'm ready for anything," I assured him while remaining totally unsure myself.

Hemingway's face had taken on a serious, rather melancholy demeanor. I could only guess that he was thinking about the past. I thought about mine. Anyway you see from around 1928 up until 1940, this place he called home had been a glorious and comfortable residence for the Hemingways, but one where the glitter wore off the gold. As Shakespeare wrote and I frequented quoted, "All that glitters is not gold. All who wander are not lost." Papa's stint in Key West during the 1930's also coincided with a dry run between the critical acclaim of his two great works, *A Farewell to Arms* in 1929 and *For Whom the Bell Tolls* in 1940. I wanted to say that we all have those "dry runs" but I didn't. I just thought it.

During his interlude here, he had experienced the suicide of his father and the birth of his sons, Patrick and Gregory. It all came about full circle here. Circles mean a lot to some folks and I thought about the Native American culture and a philosophical image of the circle in the Lakota tradition. A wise sage, Lame Deer spoke on this subject most eloquently

With us the circle stands for the togetherness of people who sit with one another around a fire, relatives and friends united in peace, while the pipe passes from hand to hand. All the families in the village were in turn circles within a larger circle, part of the larger hoop of the nation. The nation was only a part of the universe, in itself circular...circles within circles within circles, with no beginning and no end. To us this is beautiful and fitting, symbol and reality at the same time, expressing the harmony of nature and life. Our circle is timeless, flowing; it is new life emerging from death - life winning out over death

Papa had confounded the critics, but he had pleased his audience with his adventuresome experimentation. But in a sour moment, he was reported as saying, "I'd rather eat monkey manure than die in Key West." Things change I reckon.

In any case, this rather graphic quotation was attributed to Joy Williams in The Florida Keys: A History and Guide and was supposedly uttered "one summer day" while Hemingway was "sweating in the sulfurous, warm, and brownish waters of his swimming pool." I would have just called a service. I never asked him about that quote, but suspected it was possibly true, though seeing him in all his glory the last few hours indicated nothing of the sort. I can only speak for myself about the place. Key West was a glorious memory for me and while dying here wasn't a prospect to comment on, my time here had been nothing short of idyllic and well, I was already dead.

"The Soulful Passage of Tommy Typical"

Having and Having Not

"Keep away from people who try to belittle your ambitions. Small people always do that, but the really great make you feel that you, too, can become great." Mark Twain

A short time later, we were aboard *El Pilar,* Hemingway's boat, and much to my surprise and great joy, I had met another legend, this time it was Gregorio Fuentes, who was boat captain to Mr. Ernest Hemingway. He was a fine specimen of a man as well, lean and brown and he moved about the boat like a choreographed dancer. I remember reading the article about his death in 2002 on the wall of a restaurant in Chicago. He was 104 years old and had worked for Papa for almost 30 years. Gregorio was captain, cook and long time amigo to my new comrade. I was envious of that kind of lasting friendship. There remains a rather large group of people who think about such things, that Fuentes was the inspiration for Santiago, the central character in my favorite short novella *The Old Man and the Sea.* After meeting him, I may be of that group of believers.

Motoring out, I marveled at this glorious gift I had been given. This one last fishing trip. I saw these men in the moment that they lived, even though I knew their fate, it didn't change what I felt now. In fact, I began to believe that their fate had been altered in some way. Moreover *that* belief actually enhanced my feelings for the moment. All those years I lived, I had wondered how God, who knew my future, could view me right now with any objectivity. I was distracted from my thoughts when a spray of salt water doused my face. Water is reality. Fish are the offspring of that reality.

We didn't actually fish as much that day as we talked about fishing, in some ways a more noble gesture. That didn't keep us from nabbing a few tasty Caribbean fish that Gregorio saved for dinner. We live to give us a reason for eating I thought.

We had Cuban sandwiches for lunch. The sandwiches were called *Media Noches* (midnight sandwiches), consisting of pork, ham, and

Swiss cheese and then topped off with pickles and mustard on a sweetened egg bread. We also had *mariquitas*, thinly sliced plantain chips, which we washed down with bottles of Cristal beer brewed in Santiago.

As we ate, Papa told me how he had met Fuentes in 1928, and then hired him for $250.00 a month to take care for his boat. I knew from reading the later accounts that Fuentes inherited *El Pilar* and being the generous fellow that I had come to know in my short time with him, Gregorio had donated it to the Cuban government. It's now displayed outside Hemingway's former home which has been converted into a museum on the outskirts of Havana. Papa was a museum piece himself.

We had another beer or two or three as we watched the sun set in the western sky. Explosions of oranges, blues, and purples ended the day as dramatically as it had begun. The daylight melted into twilight and there we reclined, barefoot and glowing from a day in the sun. It was a spectacular day and we talked about what inspired us. I had always been told there was a fatalistic side to his nature, but if it had been there once, it was now gone some where else. Sunsets are always original, too. He was older now with the signature white beard and closely cropped hair. Somehow this didn't alarm me but instead aroused my curiosity. So I asked him personally about Santiago and he told me to talk to Gregorio. He was tired of fielding the damn question. He wasn't mad just tired. I understood completely.

Later as Hemingway slept soundly after a feast of tuna and black beans, I asked Gregorio the question and he said to me what he had said to others, "When we went to sea, we found the old man and the sea. We found him adrift on a little boat with a big fish tied there and when Hemingway went to write he wanted to give it a name and I said why don't you name it the old man and the sea?" I left it at that. There was really nothing left to talk about.

"Buenos noches, my friend," Gregorio whispered as he excused himself and tiptoed away like one of Papa's cats. I sat there alone in a quasi sleep, but I wasn't lonely. I looked up at the stars and said my prayers. I then whispered to St. Peter how great things were going. He didn't answer me in words, but I felt a cool breeze brush my cheeks and the wind said more to me in a brief moment than mere words could have in an entire day.

But a few moments later, revived, I had a ton of words spinning in my head. Since I usually carried a notebook with me, just in case I have a thought and need to write it down, upon past inclination I reached into my pocket and there, to my surprise, was a travel journal with a pen tucked inside. It was a classic diary with a tan leather cover and a cord binding and my name imprinted in gold on the front below an impressive embossed image of a trout, my boyhood Trout, the elusive one that had gotten away and Who led me across time and space. I untied the cord and turned to the first page and began to write a few thoughts about the first day of my holiday. The fat pen glided across the paper as my impressions transferred to the page and I didn't need an artificial light because the full moon in its entire glorious splendor provided the all illumination I required.

To say it had been a glorious day would have been a gross understatement. There had always been those special days when the mixture of expectation and outcome were like one of the big man's special drinks, just perfect. I laughed aloud. Then a notion occurred to me. Tomorrow when we reached Cuba, I would need clothes because it suddenly occurred to me, I brought nothing with me. Nothing at all. That's the way I came into the world the first time. So why should this time be any different?

Speaking of glorious first times, the first time I saw "To Have and Have Not"; the 1944 cinematic version of Hemingway's 1937 novel that he wrote while in Cuba, I was blown away by the exhilaration expressed by the leading role. Not only did Bogie give an Oscar winning performance, it had all of the right stuff required to captivate this young boy who loved the seedy world of pirates and smugglers. I still prefer black and white to color because of its timeless nature and its mysterious style. I was learning a lot about timelessness these days.

Though Howard Hawk's film didn't stick that closely to the book, Bogart did maintain the type of character of which Hemingway wrote and in some ways emulated. The novel reveals the exciting story of a man who smuggles goods across the Florida Straits and enigmatic Caribbean, then begins a dubious love affair. Sound familiar? Danger and romance. The critics didn't give it much praise but I liked it. That's what mattered to me.

As I watched Papa from across the table at the renowned restaurant and lounge, *La Bodeguita del Medio*, I was reintroduced to mojitos after consuming heaping portions of Ropa Vieja, a meat dish with rice and fried bananas. Sitting here at Calle Empedrado No. 206, in the vibrant forbidden city of Havana, we noshed like regulars while we talked about this beautiful island that I was visiting for the first time as I saw it through the eyes of its greatest promoter.

Florida had stimulated Papa's appetite for the tropics and here in Havana he made himself right at home. He and I had stopped off at a local mercantile where he knew the proprietor intimately and we purchased khaki shorts, loose-fitting shirts, and sandals. We had taken on the comfortable appearance that caused Martha to nickname Hemingway, "Pig". I suppose I was now Piglet, his wannabe sidekick.

Afterwards we checked into a grubby little room with poor lighting at the Hotel Ambos Mundos and Papa on a whim decided to go to a bullfight that afternoon. I explained that blood sports were generally not my bag and he said he guessed that viewpoint ruled out a good cockfight. I readily agreed. The only blood I like is in a Bloody Mary.

He grunted at my squeamish nature and compromised by saying we would spend the evening watching and betting on Jai Alai, another pastime for Hemingway who had become a stanch *devotee*. He bid me *adios* and I watched him hop into a cab and disappear into the crowded street. I hoped I wasn't spoiling his fun and sincerely doubted I was.

I spent the afternoon walking around the city viewing Pre-Castro Havana. It became a playground for the wealthy, synonymous with

"The Soulful Passage of Tommy Typical"

decadence. I read once that it had been called America's Brothel. What a heritage to bequeath although Fidel's legacy was also questionable though if I had learned one lesson so far, it was that judgment wasn't ultimately for men.

When I got back to the hotel, there was a message at the front desk from Papa instructing me to meet him at the Floridita Bar. When I arrived I saw him sitting in his customary reserved seat at the end of the bar. He was having a daiquiri and I joined him. Whew! I didn't know how much longer I could hang with him.

He talked about Marlin fishing and how the Gulf Stream offered the best deep-sea fishing on the planet. He had gotten a taste for deep sea angling while on Joe Russell's boat, the Anita, and remained hooked.

"Joe died in '41," he lamented. "He was a helluva man. A helluva man." I wondered if I was a helluva man, too.

I was caught up in the stories but the fact remained that not every thing was quite in step and that piece of information made this holiday different that any other I had been on before and I knew we were bouncing around the time space continuum like the pool balls bounce off the rail at Sloppy Joe's.

I attributed part of my confusion to the heavy drinking but I had to keep telling myself about my new state of being. Once again The Bard came to mind when he said "to be or not to be, that is the question". I was finding out that to be and not to be was the same answer. I confess that my regard for my liver had been remiss lately but I had never been dead before so it took some getting used to and was healthy living even the issue anymore? Yesterday I was at the Pearly Gates and then I'm whisked to the Keys and it's 1940 give or take a year and today I'm in Havana and it's, well, not 1941. You can see my puzzlement. If you play by one set of rules for a lifetime and then the rules change it can cause some consternation.

Papa saw my dismay and his solution was he handed me a big fat Cuban cigar that he had freshly clipped. After we lit up, he said, "Listen, Hickey, we have two weeks to cover nearly half a century and thousands of miles. So we have to break your rules a bit here and there. I am the master at that sort of thing. May be why you chose me. Am I right?"

"True." I acknowledged. Frankly, I had to admit he seemed to know what he was doing.

He finished. "So let go and just enjoy yourself. Never mind the rest."

"Okay." I stroked the scratchy beard that I was starting to grow. It felt good to rub my chin. I had a question to ask him but I forgot what it was. Oh well, it must not have been that important. I was beginning to wonder what was.

"Bring us a couple more, senorita!" Papa beckoned to one of the most striking women I believe I had ever seen and used hand gestures to place his order from a distance. "It is a beautiful place. Isn't it?" He rolled his eyes and gave a cat like smile before he blew a smoke ring that floated wistfully up toward the heavens until the ceiling fan scattered it about and it slowly vanished. I watched the smoke until it was no more.

He told me in great detail about his place here in Cuba, Lookout Farm he called it, and how he had thought it was so bloody decrepit when he first viewed it. That he saw no hope for it to be inhabitable by neither man nor beast. He smiled again. I suspect that it challenged him and that caused it juices to stir.

"But Martha saw something in that piece of decaying architecture I obviously didn't and after renting it for a while at a hundred bucks a month; I broke down and bought the place for $18,500. It's the first home I ever owned; at least that I bought and paid for myself." He thought about that statement for a bit and then continued on, "Well Martha fixed it up and added a pool and tennis court and then we moved in the dogs and the cats and I became a well settled country gentlemen, a land baron. Well at least I lived in the country. "

He pointed over his head with the forefinger of his right hand as if passing on directions, "It's about fifteen miles from here, that way, and is situated on fifteen picturesque acres. In Spanish, it's called," he paused to pronounce the name distinctly, "Finca Vigia."

I told him about my first house. It was actually a duplex. I pointed toward where I thought Tennessee would be as I recounted my past, "I visited that place almost every day as it was being built. When it was completed, I rented out one side of it to help pay the mortgage. I didn't have my own pool and tennis court, but I did buy a membership next door to a club that had one of each. I was around thirty years old at the time and after being a vagabond roaming here and there for over a decade, I know exactly how you felt, having a place to go that you called your own and settling down with the woman you love. There is a certain pride that comes with ownership, I informed him, but there is also the fear that comes with being bound to a piece of property especially if you have a thirty year mortgage."

"Precisely," he added, "Most of my characters had a great deal of difficulty dealing with that institutional enslavement."

"Not to stray off the topic, but just how long are we staying here in Cuba?" I queried, hoping he didn't mind if I moved on subject wise as I was missing that old place of mine.

"Tomorrow we fish again and then we're off to Paris." He responded. "Then after that to Spain just like Jake Barnes." He referred to one of his literary characters like he was as real as Big Skinner or Gregorio. Not only did time seem to be illusory, but also people. When we speak of people and we add our assessment, they become in our minds, that which we describe, and are reshaped in that image somewhat. And if two people are speaking of another, they become some new variation, a sum as it were, of the parts. Personalities are shaped out of thin air and it soon becomes almost unimportant as to the true nature of the person discussed or if they really lived except as an opinion.

"Sounds good to me." I said, "Almost forgetting what I was agreeing to."

Someone had tapped him on the shoulder and he apparently recognized the handsome man sporting a splendidly tailored white linen suit, who was obviously Cuban, but who spoke flawless English. He excused himself and walked over to a table where a group of multinationals were conversing enthusiastically. They all stopped when Papa arrived and turned to hear what the man might have to say sort of like that old E.F. Hutton commercial.

In my temporary solitude, I thought about "The Sun Also Rises" written by Hemingway in 1926 and the hopeless protagonist of which Papa had referred, the illusive Jake Barnes and how he and the other members of the Lost Generation were so unlike me. Weren't they? I had purpose in my life, my wife and children, my career, and above all my relationship with God. I had hope and I always expected the best or at least good things to happen. I was the poster child for eternal optimism.

Those poor souls in that book were aimless and embittered albeit in an enchanting sort of way. Maybe I was wrong. I was sure Jake's passion for bullfighting and heavy drinking with his friends, none of whom he appeared to have any deep seated feelings for, were indicative in some Freudian way of Papa. I marveled again about the person we, ourselves, create while in our temporal bodies. Was it self fulfilling prophecy or farsighted destiny or something in between, something that we know about but life in a symbiotic way?

Jake was a young expatriate working in Paris after the First World War had devastated the sensibilities of civilized people. He associated with a cast of characters that created a lot of fodder for the novel that made Hemingway an international celebrity. Gertrude Stein, F. Scott Fitzgerald, Ezra Pound, and James Joyce all played a part in some incorporated way for creating the functional mindset of the twenty seven year old writer from Oak Park, Illinois who worked diligently to shake his Midwesterner roots and become an international man.

I had traveled many miles myself to shake the perceived bonds of my own Appalachian childhood only to find that they were essential in determining who I ultimately was. Didn't he know deep inside that his roots gave him the toughness to rise above the intellectual self-importance? I caught myself trying to put some simple analysis to a complicated issue that better men than me had thought about. Since I had struggled with Psychology 101 at a state college, who was I to put some psychoanalytical spin to my host's behavior? So I stopped in my tracks and went back to the business at hand, my holiday. It was what I had right now. It was my way.

According to the plan he laid out, Hemingway intended for us to travel from France on to Spain just like Jake, the symbol of that Lost Generation and the troupe who aimlessly journeyed from Paris to Pamplona, Spain, for the annual San Fermin Festival, or "the running of the bulls." I knew that my trip, no... our trip, had some bona fide purpose. It was by design for me. That made me feel good; real good and scared absolutely shitless.

The Sun Also Sets

"The poetry of earth is never dead."
John Keats

After another long night of partying with the "Pig", and listening and dancing to "hot" Cuban music, I arose early and was greeted this time by a double shot of café cubano. We took another sea trip on *El Pilar;* the three of us, Gregorio, Hemingway, and yours truly.

We ended up dropping anchor near Cayo Coco, a little key that is a part of the Sabana-Camaguey Archipelago. It was made famous by Papa's posthumous work "Islands in the Stream". That book was a compilation of many pages of manuscript that he churned out in the late 1940's. It is a fitting tribute to Cuba and all of Hemingway's special haunts around the Caribbean, now through osmosis becoming my special digs as well.

The key was as close to paradise as there is on earth with 22 kilometers of pristine beach and plant and bird life with colors that were absolutely indescribable.

We playfully snorkeled and fished all day there and at nearby Cayo Guillermo. We took a long nap under the Royal Palm trees and after sunbathing took a long relaxing swim in what Hemingway called the "Great Blue River". It was a splendid day that becomes a splendid memory.

We headed back to Havana for a flight that left for Miami at noon the next day. Papa talked about "Islands" only because I prodded him. He had fired up another stogie and had his signature drink in hand. He created images of himself repeatedly.

"I had run out of dialogue by then. Just ask the critics. I just wanted to describe the beauty of this glorious place in between telling a good story. Thomas Hudson, my hero of sorts in that book, the intolerable painter, is a lot like me and a man has to be who he is. Doesn't he Hickey?"

"The Soulful Passage of Tommy Typical"

I closed my eyes and nodded slowly. I got the impression that my friend had also become somewhat besmirched by his own self image as the years had passed and I found myself wondering how he had gotten to that moment when suicide was the only way out especially after having lived out many days like we had just had. Maybe he knew they were inimitable those kind of days when he had hauled in huge Marlin or first hand had witnessed events that changed the world. Maybe he got used up. I couldn't understand because for me each moment of life had been precious and only became more so.

I had another Cuban cigar, a robusto size, following only a little hesitation. After all, I didn't have to worry about cancer anymore. My thought processes had gotten very strange since this death thing started or ended or whatever it did.

We took a sea plane to Miami the next day as planned. It was a bumpy takeoff but the view was fantastic as we took off and then I shall never forget my last glimpse of Havana. In 1948, my pal, wrote an article for *Holiday* magazine describing his life in Cuba. Hemingway used words as good as anyone to paint pictures. He had done that magnificently in *Islands in the Stream*, where his topographical descriptions dwarfed the dialogue. I would have to say that's the part I admired most about his writings and him. He did whatever he set his mind to do.

It was a long plane ride to Paris, but Papa was good company between naps. I would miss Big Skinner and Gregorio but felt that I would see them again someday. I caught up on my journal entries and found that the pages were filling up quickly. We had stopped off to see a tailor in Miami and picked up a few clothes and Hemingway bought me a piece of luggage. I didn't have a cent to my name and so far hadn't needed it. For a man who had worried a great deal about money, it was strange not to give a damn anymore.

Somewhere over the Atlantic as we approached the Continent, he leaned on his armrest and spoke. "Hickey, do you know what I told Hadley, my first love."

"No," I told him hoping that I hadn't forgotten some profoundly important quote from his life.

"The world's a jail and we're gonna break it together."

"That's beautiful," I said considering the depth of it relationship wise.

"We came to Paris together," he continued, "Sherwood Anderson wrote me a letter of introduction. I took a job writing for the Toronto Star. It was my start. I began working on my own style then and there. We had a son. How about you, Hickey? Any children?"

"Two, Jordan and Madeleine. They're something special. I reached to pull out photographs and remembered I didn't have a wallet. And Melanie, my one and only wife. She tamed the beast in me I used to tell friends."

"Alas my beast remained untamed in my time," he said sadly but it almost came off like a boast.

"To each his own," I retorted.

"Touché Hickey!" He exclaimed and squeezed my arm. It was the first time he had touched me. Not only was I getting to know Hemingway, now I had actually been touched by him. It felt good and I felt honored. As I basked in that moment, he had motioned for wine and within minutes, we were toasting our destination.

"Vive le France!" He raised his glass and I raised mine and the clink was joined by two other rows in the First Class section. "Ah yes," he repeated, "Vive le France!" The wine was a welcome change to three days of rum in various forms.

We had found time to take a cab to Lookout Farm the morning of our departure from Cuba. It was a splendid place and I saw exactly what he saw when he lived there. I knew now why he loved it. We stood together at a vantage point where you could see for miles and miles. As we gazed, he told me how much he loved the personality of cats. I told him I was a dog man myself. We chatted about how our lives had changed over the years. Then we left. On the ride back from the farm named, *Finca Vigia,* to the airport, he said nothing to me. At that point, he looked old. Thoreau once said, "Things don't change, people change." He had that right.

I hadn't noticed change in myself. Others seem reluctant to tell you. So you kind of drift along thinking that you're twenty one or thirty five or whatever period you happen to get stuck in. Sometimes you even dress like your best era thinking you look cool in those outdated duds. You listen to music that was cutting edge at the time but is now played on elevators. You talk about movies fondly that seem hokey when you force your kids to watch them. Nostalgia is a drug and glorifying the times of yore can be a true addiction if you focus on the superficial. Conversely if you extract the essence of it, the past can be your guide in defining the moment. I thought about Trout in that regard, that patient friend of the boy angler, who would not be forgotten. He had returned to lead me to a new stream, knowing that I would follow him. I began to think I had let him go on purpose.

My enlightenment continued after we reached the City of Light where you could get so lost in dialogue that you forgot where you were. The waiter cleared his throat to get our attention and we leaned back in our small chairs as he served us *le vin* and *le fromage.* We had been talking about marriage again, my first and only and his third that would eventually become four. The marriage to Martha Gellhorn was as ill-fated as Hemingway's two previous ones. My one and only marriage worked so well that failure wasn't even a consideration. Papa tried at first to find maturity in his mates as his first two wives had been older than he was. Martha was nine years his junior. My wife was five years my junior. So the age aspect while a fact to be considered is not a good enough reason in my book to explain much of anything. Humans do like reasons more than reason.

Now Martha was not the kind of woman it seems to want to end up as simply a housekeeper, but neither was my wife. The modern era has given women a choice and men must respond to that situation by allowing those choices to be considered. All options must be explored or one can end up with a mate full of what ifs and that can only lead to frustration. I've found that the more a person seeks to expand themselves the better partner they become. When he was drinking, they say Papa had a temper, and the drinking didn't help matters. It never does. My dad had that problem so I understand that one a little. I've also heard Ernest was quite the intimidator and by the time he and Martha married there was a degree of, let me say this discreetly, sexual incongruity, but now that's really none of my business. Is it? I'll just go on record as saying that was not a problem for me and if it ever becomes one, well thank goodness for pharmacological advancements. While we were savoring our red wine and yummy cheese at this ambiance laden outdoor café in Paris, Papa summed up his third marriage in a more succinct and less clumsy way than I had. After all, he was the master wordsmith.

"Hickey, it just didn't work out. Do you like the Bordeaux?"

I replied, like him trying to kill two big birds with one little stone, "Papa, mine did work out and yes I do like the wine. Very much. You have great taste."

It felt only natural to talk about wine and romance, good or bad, while in Paris. It was, as they say, the perfect ambiance for such things. Papa moved on gracefully to the more comfortable subject of adventure recounting his personal move from America to Europe. It was inevitable for him. "In 1921, around Christmas time, I first came to France with Hadley. We stayed nearby this very café at the Hotel D'Angleterre until we found a suitable, i.e. affordable apartment. It was located at 74 rue du Cardinal Lemoine. It took us a few weeks to land the place so we moved in, I believe in early January. In February, I met Ezra Pound and shortly after that I met Gertrude Stein. We visited Switzerland and Italy and had traveled around the French countryside and hiked throughout the Alps, all by year's end. In '23 Hadley got pregnant here. I was in my early twenties, Hickey, and I had already lived more than most men."

"Were you happy?" I asked.

"In those days I thought I was, but why always the tough questions? You must remember that I, like most, have difficulty defining that term." He thought for a brief instant. "Perhaps I was simply filled with wanderlust and having my itch scratched was satisfying enough. More baffling term, perhaps, but more suitable."

"Hmmm," I deliberated, pausing a lot longer than he had, to consider the point.

He didn't like the gap in the conversation one bit and inferred it was a judgment on my part. "Damn you, Hickey."

"That's impossible for me. To be damned that is. I've already been told I'm in by St. Peter himself and I peeked inside the main Pearly Gate." I said smugly. What a statement for a man to make about himself.

He spit out wine and laughed as loud as I ever heard a man laugh, then he exclaimed "Droll! Very droll!"

"I thought so," I chuckled. We laughed for a long while talking about the indiscretions of our youth. I told him about streaking and mooning and the crazy things I had done at rock concerts. Then I told him that I had moved on when it was time and tried to grow up. He told me that he had the tendency to stay too long and that he never quite grew up. I admitted to myself then and there, I hadn't really either.

"I learned to write in this city. I was an inspired man here, Hickey. I have been quoted as saying, 'In order to write about life, first you must live it!' That's true. How about you?"

The man did have a way to get to a person's core. As I told him about myself, I was elated that he had an interest in my story. I had lied about growing up. I had just learned a new role, the role of acting mature. But the child is always there and always has a say in things. I remember Hemingway also said, "I like to listen. I have learned a great deal from listening carefully. Most people never listen." Right now he was listening and I was talking. "Well Papa, I've been writing for as long as I can remember…"

In and Out of Season

The world is a great book; he, who never stirs from home, reads only a page. -Saint Augustine

As a kid, I begged for crayons and pencils. I composed all kinds of text even creating my own secret code and read the dictionary like it was a manuscript. Writing things down came natural to me almost like an unforced often insentient assimilation. My neighborhood was full of story tellers. From the old men who whittled in front of the local hardware to the women who talked incessantly as they stringed and broke green beans and collected the finished product in the pocket created by the folds of their dresses created by spreading their legs apart.

Almost all of the stories in my life are analogous to what I observed as a child. The sites, sounds, tastes, smells, and the impressions have varied but there is a consistency that is ever present. One such memory is of the library at my junior high school. My favorite day of the week was when my class got to visit it for an hour and peruse the shelves for a while. I was free to pick out what I wanted to learn, to go where I wanted to go within the confines of the amazing place, and to think what I wanted to think as I walked around. In fact, such intellectual adventuresome was encouraged.

There was a table where you could take your book after you selected it and begin reading it in quiet solitude, an anomaly for a thirteen year old. I yearned for such an idyllic place of my own and dreamt of having a private library one day. I had to wait, like people must do for all good things, before my prayers were finally answered and found that the dwelling I sought wasn't a physical manifestation at all, but was made of far more substantial material, the same stuff that good yarns are made of.

It began when I wrote a short story, years ago, about my personal library, not a room in my home or a building in my community or a Congressional landmark, but an unpretentious place in the most unlikely spot, the invisible cockles of my heart. A spiritual space that was full of allegorical books about me. I recounted in that candid story that was later used in a hardback of real paper and ink, that some of those wraithlike books are great reading while others are disappointing and many are, in fact, downright scary.

But undoubtedly they all belong there and are ready for me to check them out whenever I'm so inclined. All are precisely cataloged and filed in this library of me. They create quite a surprising amalgamation, dramatically different in many ways, but there is a distinctive space on each shelf that fits each book perfectly. There are many spaces for new ones, not yet written or published. The collection is constantly expanding, ever transforming."

Hemingway smiled at me. It was a big broad grin. "The way you just spoke is the way we spoke in the twenties, right from the heart. You know what; my first book was published in Paris in 1923. They printed a whopping 300 copies of my 58 page epic. Remember I also said, 'I'm not going to climb into the ring with Tolstoy.' I didn't. *Three Stories and Ten Poems* did get me a new label, however. I was now officially a Modernist. Most think 'Out of Season' which was the second story in the collection, was the finest. I don't know if I now agree or not but it did reveal my true modus operandi. I learned that prose was my bag and not poetry although surprisingly more than half the poems from the book appeared in *Poetry: A Magazine of Verse*, which was one of the foremost publications of that Modernist movement I was thrust into. I am a practical man so I made sure the right critics got copies of my book and Edmund Wilson responded by saying it was 'of the first distinction'. Edmund was a rising star and his praise went a long way in America. If I hadn't arrived, I was getting there."

"Those were the days, Hickey, the Roaring 20s, in Paris, the critical time in my career as a writer, whether I was sitting in a café, just like this one or on the floor chatting with Gertrude (Stein), I was stirred. These were great times when Nick Adams was born and Scott (Fitzgerald) was working on *The Great Gatsby.*" He was radiant. Thousands of wannabes, youthful writers with a yen like Papa have come to their Mecca, Paris, this *City of Light*, to acquire the same feeling Hemingway not only described to me, but impressed upon me and as Papa, himself once said, "If you are lucky enough to have lived in Paris as a young man, then wherever you go for the rest of your life it stays with you, for Paris is a moveable feast."

We spent the day visiting old haunts of Papa's and then had an exquisite dinner. He wanted a nightcap but I decided to stay in. I had no idea where he got the stamina. I went to my room and found my journal. I began writing about the place of which I spoke earlier for the first time in a long while. Hemingway had rekindled something in me and I wanted to write something.

He once wrote, "It was a pleasant cafe, warm and clean and friendly, and I hung up my old water-proof on the coat rack to dry and put my worn and weathered felt hat on the rack above the bench and ordered a cafe au lait. The waiter brought it and I took out a notebook from the pocket of the coat and a pencil and started to write."

I was glad that someone had stuck the journal in my pocket so I could record my words, just like him, in this milieu of creativity. I called the front desk and the bellhop brought me a cafe au lait. I was set. I had endless stamina, too. It was important to see the words on paper as I recalled the place where I retreated in my own imagination. I expect in some ways it was much like Papa's apartment here in Paris, where style and content resided, ready to be pulled off the shelf as needed. I wrote in my best penmanship taught by Mrs. McGee, my elementary school teacher who stressed the art of meticulous handwriting. I wrote about love and how if it is the first cause, then all ensuing effects will be true. I found I loved Hemingway the man just like I loved what he had written.

My Way or the Hemingway

Time Flies and Trout Flies
(Tempus and Salmo Fugit)

We met for an early breakfast at the hotel before catching the first train to Spain. It had been sometime in July 1923 when the Hemingways went to their first Pamplona festival. Having such a large time, Ernest insisted that they would attend it again and they did. After they made their third trek in 1925, he was inspired to write *The Sun Also Rises,* his first novel. That was the year I was particularly interested in and since it was my holiday that was the year it would be right now. This time Hadley would not be with him and he was stuck with me. He understood the nature of his mission which he told me was why he drank so much. "Droll, very droll," I said this time.

As we chugged away from the station, I looked out the window at Paris and then a short time later at the lavish French countryside adorned in the shades of early summer like watercolors on one of those paintings in my mind's special room. We made our way for yet another land that Papa adopted and adored, España. Spain was a defining moment for my friend as it had been for me when I first visited it years ago. I considered the importance of my first trip there.

I had broken away from a very hectic work schedule and therapeutically found myself in that paradise of sorts. The people were warm. The weather was warm. There was an air of nonchalance that seemed a billion miles away from the world of accountability. When I left the Costa del Sol for Switzerland, I was sad at the time. Equally, I was sad now as it occurred to me that my first week of this two week vacation would be over tonight. *Tempus Fugit* I thought. Time Flies and then there's Trout Flies. I have purchased 500 different varieties from little shops where one can spend hours looking at the details. Unfortunately I had become more of a shopper than a user and gave them away to more hands on sportsmen.

That old Latin saying about time led me to think about the small trout flies I used for rainbow trout when that other old saying "There is much more to fishing than catching fish," replaced my original unsophisticated childhood motto of *catch'em and eat'em.* Any releasing was called a mistake.

Many seasoned anglers still think of my home territory, the Clinch River near Norris, Tennessee, to be some of the finest trout fishing around the southern states. Trout Unlimited says, "It is a challenging river to flyfish. The clear, shallow, slow moving Clinch demands a stealthy approach, delicate presentation, small flies, and drag-free drifts. It is very much like fishing a spring creek, but this "spring creek" is over 75-yards wide! To consistently catch its wild, wary rainbow and brown trout requires concentration, careful execution, and patience."

Almost everything worth having requires those three elements I thought and I knew that Trout agreed. He rarely disagreed about important matters. He was wise but unobtrusive like John Wayne in *The Quiet Man.* Correspondingly the train ride gave me a lot of time to reflect on Ernest Hemingway's first novel, *The Sun Also Rises* again since Papa was asleep most of the time. I would not use the term peaceful to describe him but that's how he seemed in slumber as the train plugged along. His one nightcap last evening had let to another all-nighter and he was pooped. Hemingway's premiere as a novelist brought a lot of comment from friends and critics alike. F. Scott Fitzgerald said that the tome was "a romance and a guidebook." *The Sun Also Rises* produced its characters as remnants of a "lost generation." Unlike me, Papa was able to demonstrate multifaceted subject matter without moralizing. I felt I had been a part of a "list generation."

Our trip to Pamplona was exceptional though the city itself is not incredibly romantic except in the teeming medieval district. "I never liked the actual town all that much," my buddy said. We sat on a bench near the Plaza del Castillo after a lunch at a picturesque little cafeteria on the square that is the "heart of the town". We had trout filled with ham and covered in a tasty sauce. The wine was served cold and was quite good according to me, but according to Papa the chill, "...helps it overcome the rusty taste." It was hard to believe that I was in the town of the "Running of Bulls", one of the most famous events in the entire world. The experience was a part of the popular festival of *Sanfermines*. Papa cherished it as he treasured bullfighting in general, and this town was the epicenter for the sport.

We visited Pamplona's gothic cathedral, built between 1397 and 1530, with an 18th century neoclassical façade and is regarded as one of the most important religious buildings of Spain. Most valuable is its *claustrum*. In the central nave there is the *Kings' Mausoleum* of alabaster, built in 1415. I have always felt the presence of God when I visit holy shrines. Later in my life, I found out that the holiest of places were not built by human hands but by God alone and before me in this man was a prime example of that. As we strolled aimlessly, I took the opportunity to ask Papa about his religious beliefs or lack of them. He took off the straw hat he had bought from a street vendor and spoke to me.

"You know what I wrote once. 'Our nada who art in nada, nada be thy name thy kingdom nada thy will be nada in nada as it is in nada. Give us this nada our daily nada and nada us our nada as we nada our nadas and nada us not into nada but deliver us from nada; pues nada. Hail nothing full of nothing, nothing is with thee.' But before you stab me with those dagger believing eyes of yours, I also wrote, 'If a writer of prose knows enough about what he is writing about he may omit things that he *knows* and the reader, if the writer is writing truly enough, will have a feeling of those things as strongly as though the writer had stated them. The dignity of movement of the iceberg is due to only one-eighth of it being above water. The writer who omits things because he does not know them only makes hollow places in his writing.' My stories were not hollow. I was not hollow. I now know nothing is everything, too. So how about you, Hickey? What's your story?"

I thought long and hard about what he was saying and I thought long and hard about Trout, my spiritual advisor, who inspired me to write my thoughts down just a few hours before. Feeling inspired I responded. "I'm sure that your cynicism was heartfelt. I also feel compelled to explain to you something about me, in my own way, as an honest attempt to clarify my faith as it unfolded in my life. So now I shall read what I wrote in my journal on the train ride over." I reached into my pocket for my journal and I read to him. Imagine that, me reading to the great one as we leaned against a stucco building in the place that encouraged his first novel.

The Short Happy Life

What is life? It is the flash of a firefly in the night. It is the breath of a buffalo in the wintertime. It is the little shadow which runs across the grass and loses itself in the sunset. - Crowfoot

I paused letting the extended silence be like a period at the end of a sentence. Papa said "Well now, aren't you are a true defender of the faith, Hickey? Are you beginning to see the timing of all of this?" I try to explain that I honestly didn't and proceeded to raise a few questions that had been troubling me.

He stopped me and said, "Let's leave it at that for now and let's fish tomorrow. In search for both Trout and Truth, perhaps?" Frankly, I had expected a different reaction of some sort. Part of me wanted to continue to argue for my faith. But that was mere ego rearing its aggressive head and I let it pass. Most true evangelism occurs in silent casting. I paused a moment more and kindly responded, feeling what could best be described as raw passion, *sushi passion* so to speak.

"Absolutely," I said rather enthusiastically. "Let's fish."

The next morning as the sun rose, we went trout fishing high in the Pyrenees at El Burguete. Now Papa was talking a language that we both understood. I had fished similar streams near the Smoky Mountains as a kid and our expedition brought back great memories of those times. We laughed between sessions and talked more about the nuance of belief and we were very successful to boot. Proudly, we carried our overflowing creels to a local eatery where they prepared our catch for us. Having fresh trout two days in a row sure was heavenly. The wine even tasted better this time.

That night in my journal I wrote about nourishment. Trout provided sustenance for me physically and spiritually. I also wrote about the fact that belief comes down to soul. Papa had soul so no doubt he also had belief. Like the iceberg it may have been hidden for a time but now I knew the truth.

"The Soulful Passage of Tommy Typical"

I repeated back his words that he spoke while we were fishing to confirm that thought. "If a writer of prose knows enough about what he is writing about he may omit things that he *knows* and the reader, if the writer is writing truly enough, will have a feeling of those things as strongly as though the writer had stated them." I looked him in the eye. "I get the drift," I said. He nodded.

After another scenic train ride, we flew the next morning from Madrid to Milan to spend the day. Milan doesn't attract the number of visitors that frequent the premier spots of Italy, namely Rome, Florence, and Venice. But once you've had an opportunity to visit the downtown area and the outlying parks, you find its blend of past and present quite appealing.

In 1917, Young Ernest was as a cub reporter for the Kansas City Star, but that short career ended and on the morning of June 7, 1918, the 18-year-old stepped off a train Garbaldi Station here in town. He had taken on the duties of a Red Cross ambulance driver. One night, he suffered 227 separate wounds in his legs. He was shipped back here to recover, and fell in love with a twenty-something nurse named Agnes von Kurowsky. The bottom line was she thought he was too young and jilted him, then eventually found someone else. He and I had something else in common.

Ten years later, Papa wrote "A Farewell To Arms," about, you guessed it, an affair between a wounded soldier and his nurse set against the backdrop of WWI. It wasn't until the 1940s that he came back to Italy, and by then he was a famous writer, but since history often repeats itself though with a twist this time it was he, the older man falling for an eighteen year old beauty but was again ultimately rejected. The result was "Across the River and into the Trees," his 1950 novel about an aging soldier pursuing a younger woman in post-war Italy.

I asked him about war and he lamented about the aimless nature of it and used his oft quoted expression "in modern war you will die like a dog for no good reason." He grimaced when he spoke those words.

I added my own addendum," Sometimes in romance you die but it's a much slower way to go."

"Ah, Hickey, all relationships pass away. I truly loved Hadley, but in 1927, we inevitably divorced, and I felt it was improper to live in Paris since it was Hadley's city. It wouldn't be the same and I was tiring of it. So after John (Dos Passos) suggested Florida to me, I took Paula there to live and her Uncle Gus lent us money for a house. My second son, Patrick was born there in '28. I often regret that I wasn't with Hadley when my first son, John, was born. The same year he was born, I went home alone to Oak Park for a Christmas visit. I couldn't stay long. Did I mention that to you?"

"I don't' think so," I replied sensing his woe and tried to change the subject. "By the way, 'Farewell to Arms' was a great story." He ignored my compliment.

"In 1929, the year it was published was the same year my father committed suicide. I asked for the gun my father used to kill himself to be sent to me." History does repeat itself.

Everything was war with him. All of his possessions were trophies of his struggles. Not so with me. Relaxing is hard to do I'll grant because there is a great deal of strife in the world. But in my mind, I am able to separate the trials of life from the emotional ego and therefore see only opportunities for growth in life's events instead of constant battle. I loved this man but he and I were so different on the surface. But surfaces are not the stuff this afterlife is made of. Once again I thought of my past.

There was a graveyard at the bottom of a road made of rutted clay. Where the graveyard ended, there was a wide expanse of wild grass and then the river bank began. There was a stand of trees that overhang the water and provided plenty of shade. That's where I fished a whole bunch. It was at least fifteen minutes from the nearest passable road and a half hour from the main drag. I loved that spot. There was always plenty of wood for a good fire and the game warden rarely came that way. That pleased me immensely since I didn't have a pot to piss in and certainly couldn't afford a license.

Trout came back to visit me there from time to time. I enjoyed his company as I did my books for I did a lot of reading in those days and told Papa that he personally provided a great deal of entertainment for boys like me.

There was a bootlegger who had a small market that was located on a bluff above the river where I wished. I lived in a dry county and with the primitive law of supply and demand he had quite a nice little racket going there. So while most people were sleeping in the wee hours, you would knock on the back door of his store and he would come out in half buttoned long handles, always toting a shotgun and cussing like a drunken sailor. He aimed that gun at me a couple of times and though he was joking, it made me feel a little uneasy. I couldn't even bear the thought of someone else considering blasting me to eternity much less doing it to myself.

But I was not without the blight of self destruction in my family. My dad slowly drank himself to death. Toward the end I would visit him in a dark apartment that reeked of whiskey and cigarette smoke. He was an accomplished musician and he played for me the last time I saw him.

On the wall in a sacred spot beside my desk is a picture of Hank Williams, his hero, and in the band there is a friend of my dad's standing erect, looking young and cocky. His buddy had tried to convince Dad to come to Nashville, when he was a young man, but he never made it and when he spoke of it, I could sense a mixture of fear and regret. I have had that same concoction when handling some of my own experiences. Sometimes choices came down to doing the unclear thing.

In the summer of 1969, I secretly planned to attend Woodstock. I knew it was going to be a big event and earth shattering and like Jack London said, "You can't wait for inspiration. You have to go after it with a club." I was fourteen going on fifteen and I already had my plan and my backpack filled to capacity. I was going to hitch my way from Tennessee to New York and take my punishment when I got back.

But I had a decision to make. My mom was a waitress and she was working some double shifts. She came home at night and shared her tip money and soaked her aching feet. I watched her sacrifice for our family. She never complained about work. She just did her job and was always cheerful.

A few days before I was to set out, we were sitting on the front porch as was the summer evening custom and a neighbor stopped by for some of my mom's coconut cream pie. As I sat on the ground and worked on a watermelon slice, I overheard Mom told Mary Kate she didn't know what she would do without me. She counted on me to be with my baby sister while she was working.

That night I tossed and turned. By morning I concluded that like George Bailey in *It's a Wonderful Life,* I had to do the right thing so I gave up a dream and stayed at home. When August approached and the festival began, I watched the news at six each night and I was enthralled by what I saw. I bought the album when it came out and saw the movie at the drive-in and while I know I missed something that would never happen again, I also grew up a little. When people count on you and they do every day, you have to step up to the plate and execute and that's what I was doing now in this faraway place and time.

Papa had I had dinner and took a walk. Walking is such a beautiful thing. As he told me about the city as he remembered it, I watched his hands say as much as his lips. He loved to use words to their utmost potential. We stopped for a coffee and I just had to ask him what was next and he casually mentioned that we would catch a flight to Rome in the morning and then from there to Kenya.

"Africa," I shouted, "the proverbial dark continent."

"Au contraire, my friend, the continent of enlightenment," my comrade contradicted.

In my room that night, it was a time for just sitting and looking at the city lights from my opened window thinking about big little things. I was playing opera music on the radio and sipping on Chianti right from the jug when I fell asleep in my chair. I found that Hemingway somehow extracted thoughts that had been lying dormant for some

"The Soulful Passage of Tommy Typical"

time in my mind and after considering those notions, I felt I was bone tired. It was a good tired though and the warm breeze again just finished me off sending me to that kind of slumber where dreaming is not even an option and the flutter of the window curtains may as well be the wings of angels.

The approach was bumpy as our plane pitched and yawed in the big white fluffy clouds. The sky was the deepest blue I had seen since my boyhood days on top of Walden's Ridge. I was excited because I had been to Northern Africa but never in the heart of the continent. Kenya is situated on the east coast of Africa. It extends from the Indian Ocean deep into the heart of the continent. The equator runs almost dead center through the middle of the country. After our plane landed in Nairobi, we took a room at the New Stanley, a hotel "built around the history of Nairobi"; the landmark is also famous for its Thorn Tree café, where we lunched on Oysters Mombasa.

Nowhere in the world can a man find a more delicious oyster than on the east coast of Africa. The Kenyans bake them in a mouth-watering wine garlic sauce. A full dozen of the little dishes are placed on a large platter with a bowl of cocktail sauce and slices of lemon. They were good but Hemingway told me that their namesake, Mombasa, a scenic city on the coast of Kenya, possesses the very best of these small oysters.

Papa informed me that before modern telephone systems, the Thorn Tree was used "as a communications center for notices and messages from the settlers that lived in the more remote areas of Kenya."

The first time that Papa visited Kenya and Tanganyika now called Tanzania was in 1933 accompanied by his second wife, Pauline. He contracted dysentery while on a safari and he stayed for a few weeks in Nairobi where he met other men from Europe and America seeking adventure like himself. After completing the safari and returning home Hemingway started writing the travel account "The Green Hills of Africa", his nonfiction book that describes his encounters in the African bush, shooting lion and other big game. Published in 1935, it also elevated Hemingway to celebrity status.

He had connections and we took a ride in a Rover taking in a sizable portion of the Serengeti including the dramatic Esoit Olooloo (Siria) Escarpment and the concentrations of game there. Lions are found in large prides and it's not uncommon to see them hunting. Huge ranges of captivating wild animals live in Kenya which includes elephants, giraffes, rhinoceroses, and zebras.

Hunting is illegal and to protect the country's wildlife, the government has set up several national parks and game reserves. They are the best in Africa, but poachers continue to kill such valuable animals such as elephants for their tusks and rhinoceroses for their horns. We saw a Maasai village and stopped. It was apparent that Papa loved the people and the untamed nature of the land. There are more than 70 tribal groups among the Africans in Kenya. Even though the average African may have superficially drifted away from ancestral traditions, tribe is still the most important part of a Kenyan's identity.

Having a good deal of Scottish blood, I knew about the history of clans, which were tribal in nature as well. Once in America, the clan bond gave way to family relations, the bond we called it. The Lindsay's, my mother's side of my bloodline, were as fierce as their ancestors. They argued incessantly with each other, but let a stranger insult one of the tribe and watch out!

Forty eight hours of morning and afternoon game drives in the savannah along the northern extension of the Serengeti ecosystem not venture far from camp to see herds of impala, gazelle and zebra, elephant, giraffe and prides of lion. On our last evening in camp, we gather for a farewell dinner and an opportunity to review our safari's highlights around the inviting campfire.

The astonishing man no doubt played a role in creating the image of the *Great White Hunter*. Just this moment as Papa reclined against a small tree in his khakis with one knee up and the other leg extended, he totally fit the bill. He reflected, "I was probably the one who introduced the Swahili word "safari" to the English language. If it wasn't me, I don't know who it was. I trekked around East Africa twice in my life and the experiences gave me a strong background for several short stories and novels. I was probably not the greatest hunter but I had the heart of one. I dearly loved the nature and wildlife of this mysterious continent. I never learned *Kiswahili* language but I did get a working understanding of the Kenyans."

He looked over at the Land Rover and remarked about its suitability for rough terrain. "It's the best vehicle for a good adventure, Hickey"

I agreed and told him that I had owner a Range Rover myself back in the early 1990's. I drove it all over the United States racking up a phenomenal number of road miles. I loved it so much I would drive it even when I should have gotten on a plane. It took me on several fishing expeditions to the Caney Fork near the Cumberland Plateau and in the Carolina mountains near Highlands. It made numerous journeys to the Gulf of Mexico and to the Atlantic Ocean. My family in tow. Wherever I took my exotic Hunter Green adventure ride it performed well just like the one Papa had chosen for our trip here. I was like a little kid wanting to please my host and I was glad we had another small thing in common.

I continued to learn every day just how much my new traveling companion loved adventure, war and danger. A sports promoter friend of mine had once remarked that I, too, was an *action junkie*. I was flattered; for that trait gave me a chance to show off the macho image that Papa had fashioned for us. I went up in airplanes, gliders, and scuba diving with my brother. I went sky diving, white water rafting, and water and snow skiing consistently as well and ended up during my career traveling over ten million miles. Life had been good to me.

Being landlocked, living in Tennessee, I still went to the beach religiously by cashing in frequent flyer miles and rode the waves whenever I could, lying down or trying to stand up. Papa's exploits made him the *Big Kahuna* for an adventurer wannabe like me. My mystical pal and I probably differed most on the romanticism of war. I didn't stick my neck in the sand about the historical significance of it, but at heart I was a lover not a fighter. Oh I fought my share of battles but they were within me.

My Way or the Hemingway

Two of Ernest's African short stories were quickly recognized to be among the finest of his writings, "The Short Happy Life of Francis Macomber" and "The Snows of Kilimanjaro". The latter became one of my favorite movies with Gregory Peck. I have seen it numerous times. It detailed a dying man's last ponderings. Nothing is new under the sun. Using the influential power of narrative, a good many critics agree, that this was the best of his short works. The story includes the line about the rich being "very different from you and me," which was wrongly attributed to F. Scott Fitzgerald. Actually it was Hemingway's line and was first published in 1936 in Esquire magazine.

The intriguing story relates the feelings of Harry, a novelist imagine that, dying of gangrene poisoning while on an African safari. As he waits for a plane to rescue him, he intuitively knows it will not arrive in time. He appraises his life, realizing that he has wasted his time and talent exacerbated by a loveless marriage to a wealthy woman. Harry goes to sleep realizing that he will not awaken again and dreams the rescue plane has taken him to a summit of Kilimanjaro.

There, on the mountaintop called the House of God, he sees a legendary leopard just before dying. Papa once boasted that this story "put into one short story things you would use in, say, four novels if you were careful and not a spender."

I looked up at the star filled African night sky in wonder seeing mental pictures of an urbane Gregory Peck. As if he were reading my mind and capturing the same images, Papa said softly to me, "I regard *Snows* to be my finest story."

"Ernest, I believe it is one of mine, too." I selected my words carefully, not wanting to have to single out one of the many stories I preferred in particular as my favorite. I had many favorites. In fact the way I ordered them was my favorite was the one I happened to be thinking of at the time, subject to change based upon my current state of mind.

The year I was born in 1954, Hemingway came to Africa once again. He was older then and was drinking heavily. He came with Mary and they planned a safari together. He also wished to visit his son, who

"The Soulful Passage of Tommy Typical"

was living in Tanganyika. The visit came unfortunately in the midst of Kenya's Mau-Mau rebellion. It was a violent uprising against the British colonialists. Papa almost died, but it had nothing to do with the Mau-Mau. On the flight from Nairobi to the Congo, his plane had several emergency landings. Then they had not one, but two life-threatening crashes in Uganda. They survived, but were injured after the plane went up in flames. Feeling the bad vibes, they made a decision to return to the New Stanley Hotel in Nairobi.

I built a raft once and decided to float down the small creek near my home place through the center of my small town and from there I had no plans. I worked for days strapping the small logs I had cut with my own axe. I used pieces of rope and knots taught to me by my brother. I had found in the trash at a local hardware store. I conscripted a friend who worked cheap. He just liked to hear my adventure stories and get a free bottle of pop. We labored for a few days and then sealed the gaps with some roofing tar I found in our smokehouse. We smoked grape vines and corn silks in a corn cob pipe and talked like grownups as we sweated.

After stocking up with supplies which meant filling up an old pillowcase with peanut butter, a loaf of bread, a few pieces of peanut putter fudge, and a jug of water, I christened the vessel with an old milk bottle after we drug her to the creek bank. A day filled with thunderstorms had caused the normally shallow creek to rise to a level that would provide some real exciting activity. We stepped on board with a paddle made from an old broom that had stiffened after we used it to apply the roofing tar. I raised a toast to one of Tennessee's favorite sons, Davy Crockett, and after we both took big slugs from a coke, we pushed off. We made it around a couple of rocky torrents and then hit one smack dab in the middle. All of our work went down in one big crunching sound and then we found ourselves sitting on the bottom with the bluegill.

The entire voyage had been less than a minute and a half in duration and maybe a hundred yards. That sorry beginning was only one of a thousand journeys that had taken an unfortunate turn in my lifetime. The list is endless. Breakdowns, accidents, cancellations are just a few of the variables that have impeded me. Hindered me, but not stopped me. I understand exactly how the Hemingways must have felt when they arrived at a safe and familiar haven and climbed between two clean sheets and thanked their lucky African stars.

Ernest later wrote about his second safari and his trademark flirtatiousness with a young, native girl. The book is written as fiction, but most of it can be read as the diary of Hemingway. *True at First Light* was published posthumously in 1999 when the unfinished manuscript was finished by his son, Patrick.

After he told me how proud he was of his children in the end, he said we would be off for the states to visit the small town in Michigan where he spent his boyhood summers at first light. And that's what we did.

While I waited in the lobby for Papa the next morning, I saw a pretty young girl reading a book of poetry and having a cup of tea. She looked up at me sitting across from her and smiled. I saw the cover of the book and noticed it was authored by Paul Laurence Dunbar. I told her I had written a book of poetry myself and she congratulated me and told me about Dunbar. I was intrigued and she said that while Dunbar felt his best work was his poetry in standard English, he was celebrated most for his folk poetry about African Americans, written in dialect or as he called it the "jingle in a broken tongue." I asked her to read something for me. To my surprise she readily agreed. It was called *The Mystery,* and I felt it was most appropriate.

"I was not; now I am—a few days hence I shall not be; I fain would look before And after, but can neither do; some Power Or lack of power says "no" to all I would. I stand upon a wide and sunless plain, Nor chart nor steel to guide my steps aright. Whene'er, o'ercoming fear, I dare to move, I grope without direction and by chance. Some feign to hear a voice and feel a hand that draws them ever upward thro' the gloom.

But I—I hear no voice and touch no hand, Tho' oft thro' silence infinite I list, And strain my hearing to supernal sounds; Tho' oft thro' fateful darkness do I reach, And stretch my hand to find that other hand. I question of th' eternal bending skies That seem to neighbor with the novice earth; But they roll on, and daily shut their eyes On me, as I one day shall do on them, And tell me not the secret that I ask."

I thanked her and she excused herself and walked gracefully away. I suspect she was an angel. She should have been anyway. I was lost in thought when Papa appeared looking refreshed and ready for a new leg to our journey. So we caught a taxi to the airport and Hemingway proudly said that he ultimately became the Mzee, or elder, of several Shambas or villages in eastern Africa. "In Africa," Papa wrote in the book that his son, Patrick finished, "a thing is true at first light and a lie by noon and you have no more respect for it than for the lovely, perfect weed-fringed lake you see across the sun-baked salt plain. You have walked across that plain in the morning and you know that no such lake is there. But now it is there absolutely true, beautiful and believable."

Michigan

I fish **because I like to-**
• because I love the environs where trout are found, which are invariably beautiful; and hid from environs where crowds of people are found, which are invariably ugly.
• because of all the television commercials, cocktail parties and assorted social posturing I thus escape.
• because in a world where most men seem to spend their lives doing things they hate, my fishing is at once an endless source of delight and an act of small rebellion.
• because trout do not lie or cheat or cannot be bought or bribed or impressed by power, but respond only to quietism and humility and endless patience.
• because I suspect that men are going along this way for the last time, and I, for one, do not want to waste the trip.
• because mercifully, there are no telephones on trout waters.
• because only in the woods can I find solitude without loneliness.
• because bourbon out of an old tin cup always tastes better out there.
• because maybe one day I will catch a mermaid.
• And finally, I fish not because I regard fishing as being terribly important, but because I suspect that so many of the other concerns of men are equally unimportant, and not nearly so much fun. AMEN.
--John Volker,
Retired Michigan Supreme Court Justice

"The Soulful Passage of Tommy Typical"

I thought about Dunbar and Hemingway and a host of mysterious things until the cab stopped and it was time to check in for another flight. After crossing the Atlantic, we had a short layover in New York then took a flight to Detroit. After that, we obtained seats on a commuter turboprop to Grand Rapids and made the 175 drive mile north to Walloon Lake in a rental car. He talked and I drove. From the wilds of Africa to the northern peninsula of Michigan was as we would say in the South, "a fur piece." I was tired but I couldn't wait to see what the newest leg of the incredible journey would produce.

Originally named Talcott, Walloon Lake was renamed by a local butcher after he had apparently seen the name on an old railroad map. According to the local tourism guide I got at a convenience store, "Walloon Lake existed in the pre-glacial times as a river valley, which was re-shaped and deepened by glacial activity; it is the 26th largest lake in Michigan, with a lake surface area of 7.3 square miles and a shoreline of 30 miles. It is 9.2 miles at its longest point, from Mud Lake at the tip of the West Arm to the Foot, is mean and maximum depths of 28.9 feet and 100 feet respectively, and is about 100 feet above the elevation of Little Traverse Bay."

As I drove through the middle of town, I realized that it was a true slice of physical beauty, a Rockwell study in Americana, but for me Walloon Lake will always be most celebrated as the stomping grounds of young Ernest Hemingway since his family spent its summers here when he was growing up.

Hemingway was you may remember born as the 19th century came to a close. It was that time gap between the simplicity of the rural existence and the encroaching technology. His family spent most of their summers at their cottage here on Walloon Lake recapturing a bit of the peaceful life of their pastoral grandparents.

Young Ernest became very skilled in hunting and fishing. On his third birthday, his dad took him fishing for the first time. But the Michigan summers gave Papa something far beyond his enduring love of the outdoors. His recollections of Walloon Lake would be the source of the settings and characters for some of his most superb short stories.

Ernest spent most of his summers here until the age of 21, and here he learned to first write serious fiction.

Flipping through a scrapbook with yellowed pages, after settling in at the Hemingway cottage christened "Windemere", I saw a black and white image of a youthful Hemingway who looked very much like I envisioned Nick Adams, the young man who was the hero later in Hemingway's many short stories, might look. I started thinking about my favorites.

When I was a freshman in high school, I read "The Killers" for the first time. The story was about two hit men who arrive in a small town to knock off a former prizefighter. The story was published in the March 1927 issue of *Scribner's Magazine*. Papa was paid two hundred bucks for the story. It was turned into two terrific film versions. The original 1946 version stars Burt Lancaster and the 1964 version stars Lee Marvin. I lapped up both film adaptations as I had the story where Nick, an adolescent, experiences the hit men and begins his induction into full fledged adulthood and his introduction to violence.

The original title for the story was "The Matadors." Hemingway included the story in his 1927 collection *Men Without Women*. "The Killers" remains one of Hemingway's most read stories. I liked his style and the sinister themes that would occupy his work for the rest of his writing career including the emptiness of human life, male camaraderie, and the certainty of mortality, all in the form of a brusque understatement.

He claimed to have written the story on the morning of May 16, 1926, before lunch. I had been productive in my time but that was a phenomenal feat. It featured, like several of his short stories, the character I alluded to earlier, Nick Adams, an archetypal Hemingway hero, one of many of Papa's fictional selves. I got my own batch of alter egos, too.

I wondered if I was a creation of my own imagination, ego wise that is. I know that there is the eternal spirit side of me that I discussed earlier at some length but this worldly man is indeed a product of what I've seen and heard and, of course read.

In 1899, the cottage was built by Hemingway's father. I know the feeling of having a place built from scratch. There is that sense of ownership that produces a good kind of pride. That good feeling kept the boy coming back here for years later in the fall of 1921, Ernest and Hadley Richardson were married at the Methodist church in Horton Bay. After the reception was held at a nearby cottage, Hemingway rowed his bride across Walloon Lake to start their two-week honeymoon at the same cottage where I now sat. It was a place of beginnings as well as endings.

"In Our Time" was first released in the mid 1920's and though it consisted of mainly stories the collection was written like a novel, with a concrete beginning, middle and end. That compilation served notice to the literati in New York and Europe that Hemingway was a tour de force. We threw some deer steaks on the grill and he told me about his school days as we nursed bottles of beer from a local brewery.

"Hickey, I got a "D" on this writing assignment for one of my English classes at Oak Park High School. Damn thing was it was my sloppy penmanship that caused the low grade. When I slowed down long enough to make my papers legible and the teachers could read my stuff, I was "A" material. I didn't care about the grades as much as I had fun writing. Anyhow I was a good student in high school and I was editor of the school newspaper. The next plausible step after I graduated seemed to be college, but that institutional crap just wasn't for me. Eager to be self-sufficient, I went to Kansas City, Missouri, and took a job as a reporter for the Kansas City Star and well by now you can piece together the rest of the story. Shit, you blink and decades go by."

"Yeah," I said knowing first hand and that remark reminded me of something. "You know, Papa, it's been 50 years since you published *The Old Man and the Sea.* You won the Nobel Prize for Literature in 1954 and as I told you before I was born that same year. I wrote once that I was spiritually connected to Thoreau. I believe that. He was born in 1854, a 100 years before me. One hundred is a complete number. So with me a new cycle started and I don't think it is a mere coincidence that my favorite book of yours received the world's premier kudos the year I was born. That's another cycle altogether. You know my friend, there's not a better story about the big one that got away than yours. That's a legitimate reason for us to go fishing again tomorrow before our time together gets away."

"You really want to?" he asked enthusiastically.

"Absolutely," I replied.

Trout visited me in my dreams and he took me down the most interesting little stream. He led me slowly past overhanging tree limbs and under old iron bridges where you could hear the cars pass overhead. He splashed about and turned his head to look back from time to time so as not to leave me behind. I paddled leisurely in a wooden canoe and managed to keep up.

We came upon a sandy landing area and I looked around for Trout and he was gone so I went ashore and drug the canoe behind me to a secure spot and then began walking up a pebbly trail when I suddenly smelled bacon and fresh coffee. I continued on and the terrain became steeper and I could feel my chest heaving as the pathway narrowed up the inclined ground. My appetite grew as the aroma became stronger and atop a rocky crag, there was a small rustic cabin with a steady stream of smoke puffing out the chimney.

I knocked on the door and my dad answered. I hadn't seen him alive, since six months before he took sick and died. That was over ten years ago. "Hello son," he greeted me and stepped forward then grabbed me in a bear hug.

I couldn't speak. He gestured toward a table with a blue checkered tablecloth and said, "Want some breakfast?"

"The Soulful Passage of Tommy Typical"

There it was a country spread of fried eggs, crisp bacon, cathead biscuits, real butter, and homemade strawberry preserves. An old speckled pot of coffee sat on a potholder ready to be dispensed.

"Still like your coffee black?" he asked.

"Yes," I replied.

"I've been waiting for you here," he told me as a matter of fact.

"Thanks." I was still tongue tied. It had taken me a few moments to remember that while Dad was dead, so was I. Regardless we were together and that was a miracle. I suppose he sensed my consternation so he tried to comfort me with a hand on my shoulder.

Then he said, "Come over here a minute and he led me to a big picture window and it looked out over the fork in the river where the little creek joined it, my sacred place where he and I had fished so many years ago and I saw the ripples in the water where Trout was apparently thrashing about. He still lives there, the one that got away, son. He always will."

I managed to speak. "You were mad at me for letting him go. Weren't you Dad?"

He smiled and said softly and tenderly, "I had a short fuse in those days. I wanted to teach you how to handle yourself and take care of things. But I was too pushy. I'm sorry if I yelled at you. I didn't mean it. "

The old man had apologized to me this one and only time and he was sincere. He had built a cabin on top of the bluff that overlooked the spot that meant so much to me. It apparently meant as much to him as it did me. I would never have known if I hadn't died, too.

"I'm hungry," I said not wanting to make him uncomfortable.

"Then, let's eat," he said. We sat around the table and I stuffed myself. Later we sat outside on the porch steps and in the vernacular of my dad, *shot the shit.*

I woke up early the next morning and got dressed in time to watch the sun come up. That day Papa and I trolled around the lake looking for smallmouth bass, bluegill, perch, rock bass, and of course the tastiest of all, walleye. It was a good day talking about tackle and submergent and emergent vegetation.

We stopped by a local inn and had the walleye dish, pan seared and served with a rich shrimp-saffron broth garnished then topped off with toasted pistachios. We selected a white wine from Black Start Farms, a local winery. Over dessert, Papa said, "One of the finest things about living in Michigan is all the fresh fruit. Cherries, blueberries and peaches are a few of my favorites, but no one can deny the magnetism of the apple. My preferred variety is the Michigan native Paula Reds. The best preparation is stir fried with butter and brown sugar and rolled into crepes with a dollop of whipped cream and blueberries strewn all around." He motioned for the server and asked to see the chef, who readily agreed. He disappeared into the kitchen and returned a short time later with a smile on his face. He's whipping it up for us and before long we were served the dish exactly as Hemingway had described it. It was as good as he said it would be. We settled back into our bedrooms at the cottage and I thought about how life was as good as it could possibly be and just when hadn't it?

I retrieved my pen and journal and turned to a fresh page and began to reflect upon the day and then that reflection turned to other days like this one. I had a friend fly in from Oregon once and we secured a cabin at Cobbly Knob, overlooking the big hazy mountains. There we watched a couple of sunrises and sunsets and filled our hours nearby with more fishing spots than we could handle since there are over 900 miles of rivers and mountain streams only minutes away. The Great Smoky Mountains as I've said are a bona fide fisherman's paradise. While best known for trout, the park's streams are a dwelling for nearly 80 species of fish. Rainbow trout are stocked in the Gatlinburg streams, with over 28,000 trout released into eight miles of freshwater streams and the Little Pigeon River. The big question was not if but where to fish.

The weather became unruly so visions of catching fish gave way to sitting around a fireplace, smelling the burning oak, philosophizing and planning our gluttony. To close that holiday, as a grand finale, I had him sample a big bowl of an old southern favorite dessert, banana pudding. It is a gooey concoction of bananas and cookie wafers held together by vanilla cream and topped with meringue. Desserts are like sleeping pills and prepare you for a good night's slumber.

Friends and family and country cottages played a big part in my life. I could not imagine a place where they wouldn't. Was that why the Pearly Gates had appeared like a familiar wooded spot and why heavenly guides looked like Rainbow Trout?

We spent the next morning taking a short hike where Hemingway pointed out a bunch of spots that he remembered as a boy. I saw his eyes light up when he talked about them. I told him about the dream of my father. I could tell his mood changed. I remembered that the suicide of his father in 1928 disturbed Hemingway for the rest of his life and the multitude of emotions regarding the event were mixed in his troubled mind. He apparently omitted part of *Green Hills of Africa* where he damned his dad as a coward who shot himself. But he privately confided to friends that his mother, a bitch, had an significant role in his father's death. He seemingly felt that overbearing women always drove weak men to similar fates.

He never spoke of those feelings to me. He just said that when he learned the truth, evidently his position changed and the old way of thinking seemed remote and removed an unrestrained unreasonable response. In the vernacular of religiosity, I would call it repenting. I dared not say that to him. We drove back to Grand Rapids in the afternoon and caught a flight westward making a series of connections before landing in Idaho at the Friedman Memorial Airport, in Hailey around seven thirty. We rented a Jeep and drove up ID 75 known as Sawtooth Scenic Byway. It can get a little crowded on the 12-mile stretch between Hailey and the Sun Valley area but we made good time and got to the Lodge where we chose to forgo dinner instead having a small snack of crackers and peanut butter before hitting the sack.

I intermittently dreamed all night long it seemed. Dreams evoke both demons and angels and in that fantasy state you are in less of a position to distinguish them. Fortunately Trout surfaced and snatched a couple of mayflies from the top of the wistful waters of siesta then quoted Papa himself, "Never go on trips with anyone you do not love." Even in that surreal world I knew that wasn't happening to me. I halfheartedly sensed the first moments of the new morning. It was to be the last day of the grand holiday of Hickey and Hemingway. The thick well-designed curtains of my room were closed tightly except for a small little crack that wouldn't completely shut. Modest bands of sunlight penetrated through that opening, animating the airborne dust particles that one could only see when the light was shining just like it was at that moment and in that unique penetrating manner. It was fascinating to me because it was all there was at the time to capture my vision, for thank goodness the rest of the room was as dark as midnight. The hours I had been keeping the last two weeks were catching up to me.

As sleep laden eyes first open there is the blinking and the squinting followed by the rubbing and digging for the gooey stuff that might just cement them back together again were it not for a heck of a lot of hard work. Good mornings came but not without a tussle. After I was sure my blue peepers would stay unlocked, I yawned big and wide and let go a sound that resembled a swarm of opera basses singing the letter "O" in unison followed by a prolonged inhalation of all of the atmosphere my lungs could hold. This exercise culminated in a Zen like "aaaaaaaaaahhhhhhhh!" I was slowly but surely becoming awake, emerging from the most mysterious of life's marvels, the netherworld of slumber.

I was in my late thirties and unknown the first time I visited Idaho with a friend and longtime business associate. It was a playground that only God could design. The size and absolute splendor stuck in my mind.

"The Soulful Passage of Tommy Typical"

Correspondingly, Papa was 40 years old but he was already celebrated when he first visited Sun Valley, Idaho, in the fall of 1939. By that time he had written the two best-selling novels I mentioned earlier, *The Sun Also Rises* and *A Farewell to Arms*. He liked it here because subsequently, almost 60 years later, four generations of Hemingways have left their mark on the "Gem" state. What's not to like about the stark, "in your face", bucolic landscape?

Papa knew that it was his fame that initiated the invitation to Sun Valley, the new resort, which promoted and broadcasted its amenities with celebrity endorsements. The classy resort in the craggy mountains was perfect for the author and his fold. Ketchum still has Hemingway written all over it. As I recall his house is now owned by the Nature Conservancy and there's the Ernest Hemingway Elementary School and a Hemingway ski run on Bald Mountain.

Papa and Martha, his third wife lived here in this Lodge where we sat comfortably. It was named the "Glamour House" and as fitting his taste for liquor, he had a provisional bar installed. We sipped some good whiskey and munched on appetizers as he told me how he labored intensely on *For Whom the Bells Toll,* but even as he worked he played harder still, shooting, hunting, canoeing, fishing and even horseback riding and "to humor Martha, I even played a little tennis. Ha!"

He told me he came back with his children in the autumn of 1940. He had a lot of Hollywood friends, the likes of Gary Cooper and other *Big Screen* celebrities. According to Papa, Martha and he slipped away and were married in Cheyenne, Wyoming. And then the entire Hemingway family was back again in Sun Valley in the fall of 1941.

The snow had begun falling and we decided to ride out the storm by depleting the contents of his bar. "Sit back Hickey. And let me tell you about Idaho." I was all too happy to oblige. So he did. He told me that once the notoriety had ended, the family moved for a while to the easier on the pocket Challenger (now Sun Valley) Inn. When ducks on the nearby pond disturbed my friend, he and Martha moved back to their erstwhile "Glamour House" suite. On a hunting trip with Martha, the boys and some friends as they sought after antelope in the Pahsimeroi Valley of eastern Idaho, an episode on that trip was later used by Hemingway as the basis for a short story called "The Shot."

Then he was off on his adventures when the Second World War erupted. When the war was over and in addition his marriage to Martha, and not one to live alone for long, in the springtime of 1946, he married Mary Welsh, who would be his fourth and final wife. After leaving Cuba, he came here and bought a house in Ketchum in 1959. He looked tired and as he got up to freshen his drink, he asked me to tell him more abut my journeys.

I talked a while about my travels again as he listened intently. It felt good reliving those days. Pardon the pun. When I was a small fry I would beg my mom to take me to the airport in Knoxville, Tennessee. I was totally fascinated by the men and women who came and went by plane. I prayed fervently that someday I would travel like that. I got my wish and my business and pleasure took me to all fifty states and many foreign countries during my time. Traveling for me allowed all the stories from all the books and movies to come alive in me. It was the ultimate role playing exercise. It was one of the few experiences where unfavorable incidents often became the defining and most entertaining aspect of the event. Unintended consequences were welcome.

Hotels and restaurants become the memory triggering devices for those times on the road. The odd cast of characters you met became the fodder for jokes and anecdotes that amused the crowds at dinner parties and cook outs and substantiated my belief in the chaos theory. The music of the day classified the moments and the sights and sounds of your excursions replayed over and over again in your mind especially when the mundane crept in.

Ernest agreed about the threat of the ordinary. After that he told me how he tried to stay busy and kept up a strict schedule of morning isolation during which he tried to write throughout his later years here in Idaho. Then his mood and his face turned pensive as he told me how he worked on *A Moveable Feast*, which detailed his early days in

"The Soulful Passage of Tommy Typical"

Paris, his relationship with F. Scott Fitzgerald, Gertrude Stein, and Ezra Pound. Pound was actually born in nearby Hailey, Idaho, in 1885 he said. Papa then related how he also constructed a wordy story about bullfighting, which was edited and published posthumously as *The Dangerous Summer.*

"Hickey, my health got worse as time wore on and all of my misadventures caught up with me. After all there was a lifetime of plane crashes, hard work & play and a generation of hard drinking. I became certifiably depressed. I was worried about taxes and finances, those demons that get in the way of living. My personal life was always tumultuous and that phase was no exception."

He stopped talking and looked out the window and he appeared as spectral as a charcoal rendering, a mere shadow of the man I had come to know in my time with him. I asked nothing more of him that night. I looked up again and he evaporated like the smoke of the Cuban cigars he handed out so generously. He was gone for now.

I stayed in the Lodge for a spell knowing that time was put on hold in these parts when necessary. I wrote poems, my true passion, regarding what I knew about my soul with droll little notations and simple modest drawings. When I was finished, I stacked them neatly in a pile and began reading them, one by one reacquainting myself with me and wondering if the Hemingway I had come to know was really him or really me appearing as him in the second person. I'm not so sure I'll ever really know.

Filet of Soul

Who, what, if, and how
One filets the tender soul
By probing ever deeply
Interrogators one and all
Asking truer questions
I'll tell myself no lies
Why waste precious time
On all those useless alibis

Everything matters but nothing is really all that pressing except love. Don't try to teach others too much about soul, but rather let what you love about your soul speak for you to them.

Einstein said, "There are only two ways to live your life. One is as though nothing is a miracle. The other is as though everything is a miracle."

"The Soulful Passage of Tommy Typical"

Blue Plato Special

What I didn't learn while fishing
I learned at the Waffle House
While having hash brown potatoes
With my highly receptive spouse
Between bites of pecan waffles
Posed questions of great import
The age old whys and hows
In a cozy booth I do cavort

We indulged the seasoned salt
Spiced pepper of contemplation
Sealed with the blood of ketchup
Buttered up with fatty temptation
The founders of reflective thought
Mixed philosophy with appetite
And hunger with reflection
Gastronomic Greek insight

Man - a being in search of meaning. Plato
Me - a being meaning to search. Tommy

A Life Transcendent

Who are you and I together?
Who could we possibly be apart?
How inside this earthly body?
Can there be a soul without a heart?
In heaven a vessel sits empty
While on earth the temple is still
Awaiting a final consummation
Marriage of Deity and human will;
Where length is immeasurable
No gauge to splendid breadth
And moments are millennia
In degrees of glorious depth;
In a hell the essence is barren
As the intellect resides alone
All are just carnal permutations
Of futile ligament and bone;

When we die and go to Heaven, our Maker is not going to say, "Why didn't you discover the cure for such and such?" The only thing we're going to be asked at that moment is "Why didn't you become you?"
Unknown Irish Uncle of Tommy Typical

"The Soulful Passage of Tommy Typical"

My Way or the Hemingway

Find my soul skipping over oceans
and my spirit on an evening flight
sail a cruise beneath tropical moon
feel the essence of the sultry night
Red Spanish wine and mint mojitos
make my chi flow without restraint
juicy key west conch lunch beachside
my art as words on journal pages paint

Luggage packed with portable possessions
passports stamped with lifelong dreams
discovering the whole in the midst of nada
while yanking trout from mountain streams
Sometimes I have and other times have not
as distant bells toll this sun will also rise
and I am equally the old man and the sea
with papa beneath white bearded disguise

Mi papa es su papa.
Tommy Typical on the Bearded One

My Way or the Hemingway

High Times

Atop the clouds in another world
I recline and reflect
Join in repose my fellow travelers
A joyous jet age sect
Drone of turbines, unplanned jolts
Atmospheric lofty songs
Spacious world above the ground
Beyond Wrights & wrongs

I treasure you great silver bird
You lift me freely up
And provide me free soda pop
In a flimsy plastic cup
Take off my shoes wiggle the toes
Of tired tender feet
New York Times crossword solved
In the pocket of my seat

My soul is in the sky.
William Shakespeare

The sky is in my soul.
Tommy Typical on frequent flyer programs

"The Soulful Passage of Tommy Typical"

I Own My Life

Aristotle reasoned truth regularly
Locke heeded a widespread call
Adam Smith considered deeply
Ayn Rand lay bare poverty's wall
Hayek acclaimed revered verity
You couldn't keep good men down
Von Mises honored existence anew
Thomas Jefferson the spirit found
I own my life to create and dream
And to be found in freedom's womb
For the glory of the human vision
I must confront the serfdom's tomb
The art of war I must understand
Like Sun Tzu, overcome life's foe
Fly Friedman's consumerist banner
And Libertarian principles sow
When I celebrate capitalism
The innovative lucrative mind
I see limitless opportunity
God's treasures in man I find

"I think, therefore I am" Descartes

"I buy therefore I am." Tommy at Ace Hardware

My Way or the Hemingway

Skateboarding Sort

Snow can be so far away
Likewise an ocean by the beach
So I climb atop my skateboard
As the hills are within my reach

Then I will surely rock
I shall each time roll
On a board with bearings
Never forced to pay a toll

Carving turns I'm happy
I walk up to the nose
Since nineteen hundred sixty six
Have thrilled freethinking toes

My hair is thin in current breeze
Body shows lots of wear
But I am twelve where it counts
Between my ears I'm there

"That boy rides that board with wheels on it all day long. He'll never grow up" Tommy's neighbor in 1966

"She was right." Tommy in 2006

"The Soulful Passage of Tommy Typical"

Parables

I like old often told stories
I'd like to genuinely think
All those others before me
Provide me with such a link
With all that is truly human
And all that is actually just
In my quest for the ideal
They cultivate my trust
Some things are ageless
Some tales well-founded
And provide me with basis
On such yore I am grounded

"Storytellers, by the very act of telling, communicate a radical learning that changes lives and the world: telling stories is a universally accessible means through which people make meaning" –
Chris Cavanaugh

Don't let insignificant facts get in the way of a meaningful story.
Tommy Typical on seeking Truth

My Way or the Hemingway

Adirondack Chair

I like a simple classic seat
Planks smooth and tethered
And much prefer my sitting time
In a chair worn and weathered
Perusing a timeless classic
Or a basic gumshoe mystery
But if perchance I close my eyes
My reading time becomes history
Catnapping in your grasp is easy
Sipping iced tea such a tasty faire
While reclining in the comfort
Of my friendly Adirondack chair

As per the Shaw Creek General Store, the Adirondack chair was not always known by that name. According to the Adirondack Museum in Blue Mountain Lake, NY, it started its life as the Westport chair named after a small town near the Adirondack Mountains on the edge of Lake Champlain.

"A chair is a bed in the upright position." Tommy the catnapper

"The Soulful Passage of Tommy Typical"

A Scrambled Oracle

I have come to incorporate the words of Thomas Jefferson, "Your own reason is the only oracle given you by heaven."

We mix the batter
Scramble the eggs
Sometimes see fortunes
In the old coffee dregs
Dazed by what we see
Addled by what we hear
We're completely sure
That life is quite queer
But it's okay to be baffled
Rattled and at a loss
Faith throws the confusion
At the foot of the cross

I have never been lost, but I will admit to being confused for several weeks. -Daniel Boone
"...or years" -*Tommy Typical.*

Maybe the Twain Shall Meet

I have wasted far more hours
Than many a natural man
Sat in riverbank contemplation
Developing not a single plan
Daydreamed instead of toiling
Whitewashing my life away
Not a hint of laboring here
As a mind drifts off to play
When I'm crafty Tom Sawyer
Then I'm Huckleberry sane
Proud to have had the bliss
Of twiddlin' like Mister Twain

"I have never let my schooling interfere with my education." Mark Twain
"I concur." Tommy Typical, MBA
(Master of Being Alone)

"The Soulful Passage of Tommy Typical"

Inference and Transference

God is always God, and God is always what God is
God
I am what I am even when I think I am not what I am
Me
In a Universe made by God where God is always God;
Here
Then what I am when I think I am what I am will be what I am,
Now
What I am is what I am with God Together
Christ

"The knowledge of sin is the beginning of salvation,"
goes an old Latin proverb and my Mom often called
me a big "know it all" which puts a whole new spin
on the age-old ignorance is bliss argument.

My yearning has always led to my learning.
Tommy Typical 1973 at the University of Tennessee

Calls

Sometimes they bring good news
And other times they transport pain
Things proceeding right on schedule
Things just cancelled by sudden rain
They may well wake you up abruptly
Disturb you annoyingly while you rest
You can assemble an attractive offer
And confirm reservations for a guest
Or send messages about new arrivals
Bearing news of dear loved ones sick
The conveyances of an ill-timed death
You get your five rings…answer quick
Endless wired and wireless discussions
Communication empires rise and then fall
The techno human fixed on the keypad
Awaiting the forthcoming incoming call

The most important thing in communication
is to hear what isn't being said. Peter F. Drucker

"And repeating what is heard." - Tommy on bad reception

"The Soulful Passage of Tommy Typical"

Peccadillo

When I behave like less than me
Or pretend I am more than me
I seek most desperately to be
What it is that I can not be
Not content to be the spawn
But evil icon of the spawn
A product of instinct and brawn
Forsaking my spirit to my brawn
Incomplete and insincere
In defeat while insincere
And operating out of fear
In concert with what I fear
For God is my totality
Eternal law 'tis my totality
I play the game I kiss duality
Saved by God from this duality
Who I am not what I do
What I become is what I do
Time is friend and time is foe
I'm my friend and I'm my foe

Anything that seems simple is definitely not. Tommy Typical

My Way or the Hemingway

Whistle and Hum

I whistle and then I hum
Do pucker up and blow
Close it up and pulsate
Intone instinctively as I go

Don't need fancy instrument
Just my mature natural chops
Everybody can truthfully do it
Become your own Boston Pops

I carry an IPOD of good music
Inside my fleshy humming head
Within my skeletal oral cavity
My music craving is always fed

Music washes away from the soul the dust of everyday life.
Berthold Auerbach

"I bathe daily in my tunes cause I'm one dusty man-child."
Tommy

"The Soulful Passage of Tommy Typical"

St. Instant

Where was I before I came here?
Do people exist before they appear?
Is it really important that I might know?
Can I be in the dark and continue to grow?
Is a watch really helpful? Can a calendar unveil?
Could a sundial divulge what a shadow might tell?
Fossils and ruins, change of the seasons,
Distant starlight, and infinite reasons;
Like fish in the pond is my species inherent
To view our whole world via what is apparent?
When I think of God, I don't think of days
When I feel His love, it's an incessant praise;
Grace becomes real when finite can cease
And endless is fixed when Time is at peace.

What then is time? If no one asks me, I know what it is. If I wish to explain it to him who asks, I do not know. *Saint Augustine*

Time was invented by God to give my mind a chance to catch up with my soul. *Tommy Typical on schedules*

︎Library

I entered that old and friendly library of mine today that I call my soul, and after a series of rather remarkable events in the "real" world; I slumped contentedly within my spirit in that aged, restful high back leather chair with the thick cushion. Wisdom and ignorance can almost be a coin toss sometimes. I can develop a new viewpoint every time I leave the comfort of my literary existence and cast my peepers upon the wild blue yonder that directly connects me with God. This divergence is just another reason I come to this place habitually…and ironically it costs me nothing except time. The tattered book of me that I'm currently rereading is a deep and mysterious work. It is old and worn and filled with words seldom used these days, but I like it that way. I wouldn't have it any other way. Things are valued differently here in my soul and any signs of wear are seen as valuable knowledge. The tatty used editions are the most treasured. True worth is experience and not possession. The clock on the wall flashes *forever now* and I know that the wealth of nations begins with the wealth of one.

"Poetry is truth in its Sunday clothes." - Joseph Roux

"And truth is the very best outfit you can wear." *Tommy Typical on dressing for success*

"The Soulful Passage of Tommy Typical"

Tao Jones

Drives a jeep, sports sandals
Khakis and a flannel shirt
Board meetings in his garden
Weeding and hoeing dirt
Earth friendly portfolio
Enlightened investment view
Vegetarian with financial peace
Capitalist yoga guru
Votes mostly Libertarian
Briefcase is L.L. Bean
Laptop mobile office
Favorite color Currency Green
Citizen Jones reads Lao Tzu
Knows the way has no name
While he seeks his center
He loves to play the game

Kenneth Minogue says it eloquently, "Capitalism is what people do if you leave them alone," while Tommy Typical adds that the soul of Capitalism is "Selling it for a penny more than it is worth and a penny less than what they'll pay."

Top to Tip

I see without eyes
I hear without ears
I smell the danger
I taste pungent fear
Hearts pump not blood
Real minds are not gray
And I converse the loudest
When I have nothing to say
Grow up inside a wrinkly skin
Learning what is outside
By my glimpsing within
See the Lord's angels
in bright yellow flowers
The front porch is blessed
With God-given powers
Tommy 's soul connected
Without all the rigmarole
From top of his head
To the tip of his toe

"The Soulful Passage of Tommy Typical"

Holidays & Holydays

Is December really Christmas?
Or Easter, a rising morn?
Is Sunday the Sabbath?
Halloween a day of scorn?
Is January's namesake Janus?
A Roman god by the gate?
Lunch on New Year's
A black-eyed pea's fate?
Is the fourth for Odin?
"Ash" Wednesday for Lent?
Do you wait with anticipation?
As November brings Advent?
No day is really the date it is
Save April one its foolish ways
And what a calendar recognizes
Is it a particular cultural phase?
Holidays are twenty four seven
Unified with my Lord, I pray
God gives life & His promise
Each day is Thanksgiving Day!

Every day is a holy day and the celebration begins when the old peepers pop open and your inner voice yells,
"Yippie-kay-ya! I'm here another day!"
Tommy Typical on the sacred nature of every day

My Way or the Hemingway

PB&J

Some things never grow old
Or lose their mass appeal
Certain man-made concoctions
Tongue and soul unavoidably heal
Some like crust some crust-less
With crunchy or smooth PB
Strawberry or grape jelly pleasure
Variations kindly please me
Perfection inside your lunchbox
Since you were barely two
The perfect combination
PB&J and You

I would never ever completely trust someone who didn't like peanut butter and jelly sandwiches.
Tommy Typical on the best sandwich in the world

"The Soulful Passage of Tommy Typical"

God Sense

I saw God earlier today
When my son said, "Dad, let's play!"

I felt God late last night
While on a bumpy red eye flight.

I tasted God for heavens sake
As I forked a banana pancake;

I heard God all the times
I read my daughter nursery rhymes.

I smell God with my big Irish nose
Every time I sniff a blooming rose!

"People can be divided into three classes, the few who make things happen, the many who watch things happen, and the overwhelming majority who have no idea what has happened" wrote an anonymous sage. It all begins with a choice to see the Divine in the world around you. Then take notice and angelic messages will flood your senses and an invisible halo will surround your old noggin.
Tommy Typical 1987

Walking in Paradox

As a boy, I was reminded of death each time I passed the local funeral home with my fishing pole in hand. Someone was usually lying inside ready to move on to a bigger fishing hole than mine. Like many aspects of being human, that, too, made me happy and sad at the same time. That hasn't changed.

> Begin and end
> Stop and go
> Eternity unfurls
> Universal flow
>
> This day unconsidered
> This moment unplanned
> One last falling grain
> Of the hourglass sand

"You don't get to choose when or how you're going to kick the bucket but where it's going after you do,"
Tommy Typical on life and death

"The Soulful Passage of Tommy Typical"

Losing Count

How many times have I opened a can?
How many times have I lifted a glass?
How many times pulled on my ear?
How many times pumped myself gas?

How often have I cleared my throat?
How often have I combed my hair?
How often have I popped my knuckles?
How often have I taken a dare?

I lose count of my movements.
I lose count of my monkey ways.
I lose count of the stars in the sky.
I lose count while pass my days.

Life is a series of calculations, so many in fact that we lose count of the counting…so count your peck of troubles if you must count something because you couldn't even begin to count your blessings. *Tommy Typical on the math of gratitude*

My Way or the Hemingway

Oak Tree Constitution

I went to the old nursing home
To visit a sweet aunt that I adore
Raucous young lass grown old
A gray lioness lacking her roar
Slumped in the aged wheel chair
Shaking hands brushed her lap
An oak tree of a constitution
Nowadays devoid of its sap
But those eyes held that something
Though the body could not produce
Beneath the furrowed trembles
An eternal spirit wanted loose

Do not regret growing older. It is a privilege denied to many. Author Unknown but suspected to be Tommy's Aunt Jackie

What I am is God's business.
What I turn out to be is my work.
Tommy Typical's motto from Vacation Bible School

"The Soulful Passage of Tommy Typical"

Mustachioed Harvest Gypsy
A Steinbeck Moment

I'm a New Millennium Okie
Seeking the Promised Land
Straddling The Red Pony
Near ancient Pacific sand
Where all The Grapes of Wrath
Poured as idealist's Beaujolais
At taverns on Cannery Row
In seaside village dub Monterrey

East of Eden this California
There I be of Mice and Men
Define the Pearl my America
Through John's unstinted pen

Me an impatient longing mongrel
The self sufficient alley cat
Who touches the great unknown
At this juncture by Tortilla Flat

Waves and Waves

Life is, in one regard, defining your four corners, and then filling in the space with something tangible so that you can define it in some distinctive manner. God, I am sure, will help us redefine it in a larger fashion, some day, but for now, we must do the best we can. Reflection is a good and worthy use of time because it is the little things that fill our spaces.

> I wave a salutation when I pass you
> And I wave you off when I mean "no"
> We wave goodbye when we part
> I flutter my fingers to wave hello
> Big wave at weekend football game
> Sad wave the first day of school
> When I execute the cannonball
> Make a wave in the swimming pool
> We waive our basic legal rights
> Some hair wave is considered nice
> We listen to new wave music
> But riding waves, that's my vice

I'm one-third solid and two-thirds liquid soul.
Tommy Typical on why he loves the water

"The Soulful Passage of Tommy Typical"

Oh Boy! Oh Joy!

Flutter little wings
Clutter little minds
Mutter little words
Stutter little lines
Divide the spoils
Decide one's joy
Divorce mundane
Divine little boy
Pedal to heaven
Metal and skin
Poppin' a wheelie
Ride like the wind

Nothing compares to the simple pleasure of a bike ride.
John F. Kennedy

And no accomplishment greater than popping
a wheelie while on a bike ride.
Tommy Typical on his boyhood ride

My Way or the Hemingway

Do the Math

Quotient gave me
Piece of heart
Sum of life
Totaled part
Subtract pain
Square the joy
Infinity rules
Figures this boy
Geometric growth
Algebraic path
Exponential thrill
Do God's math

$$2 \times 8$$
$$\div 6$$
$$2\sqrt{12}$$
$$\overline{1, 2, 3 \ldots}$$

The laws of nature are but the mathematical thoughts of God.
Euclid

Make a bad grade in math and the law of mom became clear.
Tommy Typical

"The Soulful Passage of Tommy Typical"

Company

This old man he loved me
In ways that I would not agree
In a flashback
left in tact
That won't leave the boy alone
This old man is here yet gone

It was two days before the big 1961 Fourth of July celebration at my hometown's baseball field. I was almost seven. My dad took me fishing and he talked about the skill of Roger Maris not yet knowing the Yankee would hit 61 homers that year. There was a "Y" where a small creek poured into the river. I still visit that place when I get back there as my Walden Ridge is as sacred as Moses' mountain. There I hooked a rainbow trout and I brought him in, well almost. I had him in my grasp and Dad said to hold him still while he brought the stringer over commenting that he was about a hand and a half, a good size Rainbow. It was my first.

I held that fish for a moment and I got a good look at him and him at me. Then he wiggled his slippery body and turned simultaneously and I lost control of him and he got away as I helplessly watched in disbelief. My dad launched into one of his red-faced tirades where each sentence was completed with the word, son. I was no longer there as I just watched the water as it splashed and then the ripples abated and the fish was gone. But I never forgot him. I never will. That moment is just as real decades later as it was when it first happened. I remembered everything about him and how he swam in front of me and in between his gyrations; I still see him smiling in that trout-like manner in my mind. I even now recall how it was to encounter him. He was the one, who helped me see that everything was also something else. No mere fish could produce such feelings. Could it? Or was it like those Jack London stories where I got to observe the multifaceted levels of God's world in the seemingly commonplace aspects of living? That trout helped me understand who Jesus was in a unique way. He took the highest levels of my belief and turned them into knowing for me. That what I wished for could be as good as I hoped. I knew the trout was not meant to be caught but instead to remain mysterious and illusive and all the more lovable for it. I smiled at my dad in genuine appreciation for his part. He wouldn't be mad for long for I knew the power of my smile and my silence. That's how I frequently defused him and later in life, I used those same techniques to sell things and earn my keep & buy tons of other experiences. "You're something else," he use to growl at me. "If you only knew," I'll say to Dad when I catch back up with him in another place, "If you only knew." These days I find that I really miss that growl. A lion wouldn't be a lion without it, I suppose.

"It doesn't matter who my father was; it matters who I remember he was." Anne Sexton

"What I remember is in the end my choice." –Tommy

"The Soulful Passage of Tommy Typical"

Sunday Morn

I awaken and greet this day
A new Sunday morn hello
Hummingbird makes her music
As a neighbor starts to mow
Faraway I hear a barking dog
See a squirrel climb a big oak tree
The first day of the Lord's week
Is just peachy keen with me

"On the eighth day God created coffee!"
Tommy's unknown friend at Starbucks

On the eighth billion day man created the Mr. Coffee Maker
...Tommy Typical on the miracle of kitchen appliances

My Way or the Hemingway

Near Misses

Yellow lights
Icy patches
Slamming doors
Short-stemmed matches
Kiss and tell
Bait and switch
Fraying ropes
Loose trailer hitch
Halley's Comet
Hurricane path
Overhead obstruction
Nature's wrath
What might be
What could have been
What ifs and buts
Irk mortal men

Luck is man's ignorance of God's ways expressed
as an acceptable four letter word
Tommy Typical on arriving in Las Vegas

"The Soulful Passage of Tommy Typical"

Crossword-itis

Down and across
According to theme
I rip my paper apart
Headlines can wait
And Sports can, too
The puzzle has my heart
Jog my memory
Sharpen my wits
Count each letter aloud
When I see no empty slots
I relax, spent but proud
If National or the local rag
Doesn't matter much at all
At times I zip through 'em
Other times I hit a wall
Regardless I have high esteem
I am not a egghead nerd
And I have no cross terms
For my beloved cross word

Egotism, n: Doing the New York Times
crossword puzzle with a pen. Ambrose Bierce

Real Egotism is without my reading glasses. Tommy

My Way or the Hemingway

Ice Cream Dream

I like ice cream
Have all my days
I like it served up
In hundreds of ways
As a milk shake
Or scoops in a cone
Adrift in a float
In a bowl all alone
Tons of flavors
But vanilla's alright
A sundae on Sunday
Sates my appetite
Big banana split
Parfait with a cherry
The ultimate means
To sample God's dairy
Store bought is good
Drive through in a rush
But homemade is best
For this ice cream lush

"Grasshopper, when you can eat the entire cone without dripping on the sidewalk, it will be time for you to go."
Tommy Typical at Baskin and Robbins

"The Soulful Passage of Tommy Typical"

Grow

Grow
You must grow
You have no choice
Speak
You must speak
To hear your voice
Live
You must live
To live you win
Die
You must die
To live yet again

"The day the child realizes that all adults are imperfect, he becomes an adolescent; the day he forgives them, he becomes an adult; the day he forgives himself, he becomes wise." Alden Nowlan

"I am working on wise." Tommy at fifty

Lake Side

There's a place where peace abounds
A red clay shoreline splendid
Where sunsets are beyond belief
Tinted by cherubs descended
Meteorites in summer sky
Bass jump in hooked ballet
Canoes skid across the wake
Butterflies flutter in play
On a smooth stone I reside
To sense perfumed vines
As a June bug journeys
Among unprocessed signs
Speaking spirit words
Hearing eternal timbre
Feeling immortal hints
I at last do remember
When I come to lake side
Soul and matter meet
My soothing Father in unity
Matrimony ever sweet

If there is a little bit of truth in everything, then everything has some truth to reveal. I call that *peek-a-true. Tommy Typical 1974*

"The Soulful Passage of Tommy Typical"

Ukulele Vanished

What happened to you, ukulele?
You brought islands home to me
And entertained my true essence
Underneath the big palm tree
From your teeny russet body
Sweet sounding guitar's brother
Your pineapple aloha harmony
Your melody is like no other
Old landlocked landlubber
Dreams of that one vacation
Nashville Kahuna commiserates
'Bout misplaced 4 string elation

Ukuleles, bongos and kazoos are grossly underrated musical instruments. I recommend owning one of each.
Tommy Typical on surveying his office

Goodbye in any Language

Either way you happen to say it
To get out it is the way
How you happen to get there
Is just not for me to say
Departure prompts excursion
Emergency triggers motion
At the moment proceed like Moses
And leave your Land of Goshen

Goodbye started out prior to the 16th century as the phrase "God be with you." That's what I still mean to say when I say it.
Tommy Typical on Farewells

"The Soulful Passage of Tommy Typical"

Bullfrog Speak

The river narrows nears the riffles
Little pockets of aqueous oration
None is more enticing my friends
Than that amphibious postulation
Bass ensembles gather routinely
To liven up a midsummer's night
They sing and talk and often chant
'Til the allure of dawn's initial light
As I camped on the western bank
Crackling fire the solitary noise
The bullfrog spoke to me alone
Just a croak between us boys

Bodysurf

Surfboards Boogie boards, good fun all
Koa boards, fiberglass, all heed the call
When kid sees horizons, water and sand
Starfish call together mammal from land
These days au natural me and the wave
  Soothe the intellect oceanic knave
  I do my gliding as Neptune's son
  The body & board merge into one

I recalled gleefully how bodysurfing is one sport that you can perform just for the shear fun of it! I remembered the first time I stepped into a pair of borrowed fins and found some waist high waves to practice on near Panama City, Florida, the Redneck Riviera, when I visited my sister who lived in southern Georgia at the time. You can bodysurf either breaking waves or waves that have already broken. It's your choice on how you become one with the sea. We humans are just along for the ride any old way you look at it. *Tommy Typical Spring Break 1976*

"The Soulful Passage of Tommy Typical"

Sticky Stuff

Silvery sticky
Functional film
Carry a roll or two
Mend the things that
Crack or break
Patch them up
Like they're new
In your suitcase
Old gummy amigo
Ready to wrap and roll
In your tool box
Essential one
Repairs a
Broken soul

"My physics teacher taught me more about nothing than I'll ever know about everything else."
Tommy Typical Junior in High School 1970

Simultaneous Combustion

While John and Yoko sang from bed
The third rock turned upside down
Me and beagle fished by a stream
On the outskirts of my hometown

Now way over there in Amsterdam
Lennon's were protesting in the buff
As I was angling for a rainbow trout
Underneath the steep clay bluff

War prolonged in some faraway land
While I skinny dipped in the creek
And sang my favorite Beatles' songs
Instant karma boy & dog might seek

The '60's were a chaotic time for both the world and me.
But good grief what decade hasn't been?
Tommy Typical in 1989 reflecting on 1969

"The Soulful Passage of Tommy Typical"

A Few Things

My body and spirit
now fully agree
There's many things
that I can not see
I'm completely open
to the possibility
There's a little bit more
clandestine in me

I talk often of things I have owned in my life that meant something to me like my first Barlow pocket knife. I lost it and I miss it. Before I did I learned to whittle at the old grocery store on the corner of Creek and Chestnut Streets. I think about lost things a lot and I'm convinced that some things are meant to be lost. Preacher Baird used to talk about how we had to lose our Lord on the cross in order to find the salvation offered by God. I didn't fully understand that at first, but as the years have past, I see what he meant. My soul pants for what is missing.

Mr. Mark Twain wrote of the American classic knife in The Adventures of Tom Sawyer, "Mary gave him a bran-new Barlow knife worth twelve and a half cents; and the convulsion of delight that swept his system shook him to his foundations. True, the knife would not cut anything, but it was a "sure-enough" Barlow, and there was inconceivable grandeur in that - though where the Western boys ever got the idea that such a weapon could possibly be counterfeited to its injury, is an imposing mystery and will always remain so, perhaps."

Well, mine was sharp enough that I cut the fire out of myself the first day and my tutorial was from the owner of the store who told me that he bet I wouldn't do that again and I didn't. That's how things were taught in those days. Wasn't it? Mr. Twain pontificated further in the Adventures of Huckleberry Finn, "All the stores were along one street. They had white domestic awnings in front, and the country-people hitched their horses to the awning-posts. There was empty dry-goods boxes under the awnings, and loafers roosting on them all day long, whittling them with their Barlow knives; and chawing tobacco, and gaping and yawning and stretching - a mighty ornery lot."

I will never forget my first chew of tobacco and how I had initially felt euphoric before turning a shade of baby poop green according to one of my teammates. Then I puked my guts out after deserting my post at first base for the Davis Mills Little League Baseball Team. Like Orson Wells remembered his boyhood sled, Rosebud, I remember a few of my favorite things like my old backpack I purchased from the army surplus store, filled with many valuable things like sisal rope, tape, glue, a hatchet, a bicycle wrench and tube repair kit, and a box of stick matches kept dry in a plastic bag so I could build me a fire out of the driftwood on the shores of Norris Lake if I needed to. Those things have been transformed from what they were to what they are and what they are sustains me today in a far more significant way than they did in those days.

"The Soulful Passage of Tommy Typical"

Fidget and Wiggle

Squirm and fiddle
Can't get just right
Twitch in the neck
Jeans are too tight

Shift and stretch
Straighten and slump
Cheek to cheek
Boxers in a clump

Charley horse
Knuckles crack
Big old itch
In the small of the back

Lick the lips
Rub the nose
Rotate the ankle
Wiggle the toes

"The human body is a snapshot of the soul."
Tommy Typical on being nervous

Screen Door Metaphor

After walking across the front porch
Through the squeaky screened front door
That always slammed when you let it go
As you stepped on the hardwood floor
The mosquitoes could not penetrate it
Birds were forced to remain outside
Only chosen biped Homo sapiens
In this clapboard abode reside
I used to watch the thunderstorms
Through the mesh saw lightening flash
Eavesdropped on my teenaged sister
Whilst her lover whispered unabashed
Most often it was left unlocked
Still there was a pointy latch
That slipped quite easily into
A receptive eye bolt catch
Safety and comfort therefore within
Beyond the portal reservations wait
Thin layers of the patterned wire
The hardware employed to separate

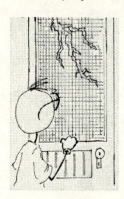

"The Soulful Passage of Tommy Typical"

What's in a name?

You may call me what you will
Or what's written on the card
The name in the phone book
Or the sign in my front yard
I want you to really know me
By a completely different tag
There was a time I was the "zig"
Now I'm sure that I'm "the zag"

I am known by many names. You can be many people in your life and still be the same soul. That's my thinking. Now because of the passage of time, I have done a lot of things and every activity has produced a "good tired" and I have often considered the prospect that death may be just a short catnap before beginning a new life and I am quite sure that there will come a time when God will call me by my <u>real name</u> and I will answer to it as if I knew it all along.

Fate tried to conceal him by naming him Smith.
-Oliver Wendell Holmes, Jr.

My Way or the Hemingway

Harried Moose

I've got to do this
I've got to do that
I've got to run errands
I've gotta let out the cat
I've run out of time
I've run out of bread
I'll run out of options
I'll run 'til I'm dead
I want a "do over"
I want a new day
I want to rewind
I want to replay
I moose be here
I moose be there
I moose be ready
I moose fix my hair

I used to hurry up and wait. Now I sort of wait up to hurry. *Tommy Typical 2002*

"The Soulful Passage of Tommy Typical"

The Bar of Soap

I've crawled the finest pubs
U.S. and the British Isles
Confirm that for yourself
The CIA has lots of files
The tavern that's the greatest
Well might be on a rope
For when I need a lift
I visit the "Bar of Soap"
Lathers nicely in the shower
Or in a steamy sated tub
Gently over epidermis
After a healthy scrub
So when Happy Hour's due
Don't be a dirty dope
Visit the waterin' hole
Frequent the "Bar of Soap"

"Some folks can look so busy doing nothin' that they seem indispensable."
Kin Hubbard

"Make mine a double shot of "lye" soap that is." Tommy in the shower

Body Indentions

Small of the back
Pit of the arm
Roof of the mouth
Just to name three
Below the ear lobe
Arch of the foot
Lines on the knuckles
Bend of the knee

Both of the temples
Atop the round cheeks
Speaking of which
The crack of the butt
No need to look far
No need to look hard
Or there's a chance
You find yourself in your rut

The greatest places I've been can't be found on any map.
Tommy Typical on the roads most traveled

Lifts

Go upsy daisy
by elevator
in a booster seat
or an escalator
You give a hand
Hoist up the sail
Raise expectations
By the U.S. Mail

"The acid test of a passing thought, a single word, a broad statement a comprehensive philosophy, a religious body, or a world view must begin with Love as its first cause or it will in the end be invalidated by the effects of its own actions be it in a split second or in eons." *Tommy Typical on the "Truth of Love" which lifts his spirit every day.*

Uncle John the Baptist

My uncle John was a preacher man
King James Version through and through
Lived a life and walked the walk
Had his name on a first row pew
Sinewy gent with big strong hands
Country twang from loving soul
Spoke of tender savior Jesus
Who could fill your god shaped hole
In the heart of mortal men he said
The lord would live and bless
He promised like his alter ego
Two men crying in the wilderness
I struggle with faith and reason
A man molded from primeval mud
And I'll pray with humble gratitude
It's John the Baptist in my blood

"In those days came John the Baptist, preaching in the wilderness of Judea, and saying, Repent ye: for the kingdom of heaven is at hand." The Gospel

"The Soulful Passage of Tommy Typical"

Pup Tent Content

From the hills of Pellissippi
To the depths of Walden Ridge
My canvas well staked home
My water tight covered bridge
A sheath under my flannelled back
And a goose down sleeping bag
Made me like a green cocoon
Twixt poles with some midriff sag
I see each and every stitch
Hear the raindrops pitter pat
Smell campfire's embers dying
I sleep better in my Yankees hat.

Pancakes

Round browned batter
Smothered in butter
Soaked with syrup
Me digs right in
Toss on banana
A slice of bacon
Sausage will work
Precursor to grin
Morning delight
Greet the new day
Cakes on the griddle
Kitchen smells fine
Love Aunt Jemima
And this tasty creation
Heaven on a plate
Sweet breakfast sign

A banana pancake is not to be taken or eaten lightly.
Tommy Typical

Tree House Memories

Scraps of lumber reinvented
Tall oak as high rise host
Rope as knotted elevator
The Swiss family's latest ghost
Shoe box of baseball cards
Nail hanger for catcher's mitt
Room for one to stand up tall
And space for one to sit
There second string linebackers
And future fathers yet to be
Practice the art of belching
High in a backyard tree

My Way or the Hemingway

Good ol' Sushi Boy

You can fry it or grill it
Or bake it or sear it
I like mine fresh and raw
Rolled with rice and crunchy filling
I stick it in my craw
Orangey pinky white or grayish
Fish as human bait
Shaped by the man
With the puffy hat
Artwork on my plate
Finger food with ginger side
Soaked in sauce of soy
Way of eating eastern style
For southern good old boy

When Jose Simon said, "In Mexico we have a word for sushi: Bait".

"Most from my hometown in Appalachia would agree with him. But once you try it, you are hooked, so I guess it is bait after all."
Tommy sitting at Kabuto's with a Kirin in hand.

"The Soulful Passage of Tommy Typical"

Packing

Zippered compartments
Shaving Kit filled
Lids on tightly
Recall past things spilled

Socks inside out
Outfits in tact
Layered by order
An organized fact

Portable closet
Human needs space
Carry-on luggage
Life's a suitcase

Photographic Images

I see me in various ways
In sundry poses
A wide range of days
See me in specs sometimes not
With and without wrinkles
Seasons cold Seasons hot
I see me in styles old and new
Intelligent looks
Those devoid of a clue
I see me a bit overfed
Alert and alive
But I can't see me dead

"Sometimes I do get to places just when God's ready to have somebody click the shutter," wrote Ansel Adams and Tommy Typical says "Life is a Kodak moment."

"The Soulful Passage of Tommy Typical"

Miracle Spread

At the heart of hope is the belief that miracles are real. If I cease to believe that miracles can occur, then the child in me is on the run and my innocence is finally lost.

If a plane can fly
Or a baby be born
Why not find a miracle
In exploding popcorn?
If Halley's Comet returns
And if bees make honey
Why not believe
In a big Easter Bunny?
If you live on a big ball
Heated by a small star
Why not imagine
You could shoot par?
If tetanus is over
If Polio can cease
Isn't anything possible
Like maybe God's peace?

Here's the deal, to paraphrase Einstein,
It's all a miracle or nothing's a miracle.
Tommy Typical while spreading Miracle Whip on a BLT

My Way or the Hemingway

Barney Blarney

My sister's cat named Barney
Liked to pee in my shoes
That action really frosted me
But I was merely paying dues
You see I'm a canine person
It's big dogs I most adore
And I spoke harshly to that cat
Whom I endeavored to ignore
No timely petting received he
From his master's elder brah
Instead meows left unanswered
Each day was my rude hurrah
A slob I left chest drawers open
Then I reaped what I had sown
My pj's as feline's sleeping spot
The cat's pajamas were my own.

"Never ever piss off a cat."
Tommy Typical on survival

"The Soulful Passage of Tommy Typical"

Grouchy

I have chosen to be grouchy
And my mood is quite foul
Both surly and inauspicious
I grunt and then I growl
I work on my grumpiness
I bark and then get all red
So quick to turn on you
And all you have said
Underneath, the "real me"
Is really quite mystified
The sunny self who's me
Was once again denied

"A Grouch escapes so many little annoyances that it almost pays to be one," Kin Hubbard reflected. We all relish our moments of grouchiness because we become the center of attention like when you throw a tantrum or hold your breath. The trouble is while you are being a Grouch nothing changes except you. Thank God that God isn't grouchy!

My Way or the Hemingway

Frosty Feet

Warm weather liberated spirit
An old barefoot Parrothead
Who likes no socks or shoes
I'm under worked and overfed
When the holiday season comes
Uncovered ankle always knows
When I get a case of frosty feet
And those frozen Popsicle toes
I stow my trusty sandals
Kiss my flip flops goodbye
Slip into a pair of boots and
This cover up makes me cry
Summer tan fades too quickly
Casper skin tone now I see
As I shelter my free birds
A chilly covered destiny
After schussing down a mountain
The old limbs will surely tire
In the lodge the boots come off
Expose my old dogs to the fire
And pretend that it's August
By a beach with drink in hand
Old soles and soul exposed
Little piggies playing in the sand

"The Soulful Passage of Tommy Typical"

August

Everyone likes a picnic
Eat in the open air
Sharing food and banter
On the way to the County Fair
Potato Salad sweet Cole slaw
Fried chicken and layered cake
Water skiing and sun bathing
A big old chocolate shake
A pick-up game of softball
Sprinklers after dark
Listening to Chicago
Sing *Saturday in the Park*
Hot and muggy days
Sweltering sticky nights
Pull into the driveway
See the front porch light
Settle between cool sheets
Ice water on night stand
August days like this one
Forever in demand

"Deep summer is when laziness finds respectability"
Sam Keen

Slinky

I bought myself a Slinky
Watched it slink back and forth
Skulked to the South
Sprung to the North
A toy for both sexes
The advertisement states
When you extend it outward
Comes home without long waits
Buy your fancy gadgets
I indulge my own doodad
And stick with metal coil
As my mind's mindless fad
I take a recurring journey
To a Christmas most profound
When stuffed in my stocking
A Slinky this young boy found

"We don't stop playing because we grow old; we grow old because we stop playing." George Bernard Shaw

"The Soulful Passage of Tommy Typical"

Wooden Things

Baseball bats
Porch swing slats
The spoon to stir the tea
Window frames
Old peg games
The pier by the sea
Lincoln Logs
Holland clogs
A pencil painted yellow
God's timber hew
On the front row pew
A peg-legged happy fellow

"Before enlightenment; chop wood, carry water. After enlightenment; chop wood, carry water." Zen Proverb

Beach Towels

I performed an exercise late last week
My frontal lobe I commenced to tweak
Found memories of beach towels past
Those earthly things not meant to last
Several striped ones yellow and blue
A polka dot solitary with a pinkish hue
Hip designer brands with monograms
Smooth and soft touching my gams
Most were stained with suntan lotion
Two hijacked by the grasping ocean
My woven fabrics contained a vault
A chronicle of life's sand and salt

There's nothing like stepping out of a refreshing shower and wrapping up in a big soft, sweet smelling bath towel. Besides as Dave Barry says, "The only lower-body garments I own that still fit me comfortably are towels.

"The Soulful Passage of Tommy Typical"

Order in my Universe

I want law and order
In the midst of this chaos
On all my rolling stones
I don't expect to gather moss

I stretched trying to recall a few Tai Chi movements. I heard popping and cracking and I repeated the unfolding exercises until the din ceased. Starting with my neck and working my way down the arms and knees ending my ritual with a big resounding snap as I flexed my ankles. Rice Krispies had nothing on me. I realized it was time for that long walk to the bathroom and I made the journey in record time taking only a minute and a half to creep the ten feet to the toilet. I leaned against the wall with one hand for balance as I smacked my dry lips and made an attempt to clear my throat, which was a little bit sore from the constant drainage caused by a rhinovirus or the fact that I had spent the day before hanging out in sub-freezing temperatures on top of Heavenly at Lake Tahoe.

After I finished my morning business, I adjusted my flowered boxers and turned around to face the sink and the illuminating mirror above the washbasin. The lighting in my bathroom is that bright revealing sort that shows oversized pores and magnifies the length of nose hair. The whites of my baby blues were road mapped with red lines. I turned on the water and after splashing several handfuls of cold water across my face; I begin to feel in control of my destiny once again. I turned on the shower and waited impatiently for the water to achieve that perfect temperature somewhere between warm and scalding. The steam rose around me as I stepped from my shorts into the watery bliss and soaped my body from head to toe. I applied shampoo, then conditioner on my mane and rinsed for an indeterminable period of time thinking of absolutely nothing if that's possible. I toweled off listening to the morning news on the old radio that had withstood the hostile environment of the condo's nightstand. My cottonmouth was abated with mint toothpaste and a vigorous brushing that caused the gums to tingle in an invigorating way. The probing of the floss and a quick rinse with the complimentary bottle of mouthwash completed my oral work out. I had ceased combing my hair preferring to run my fingers through the short cut to save time. A little extra water and a wee bit of gel and that's all she wrote. The entire shaving process having been eliminated since I now sported a grey beard that I found I either liked or had simply rationalized my laziness. I had rediscovered the eternally pleasing feel and aroma of a splatter of that simple cologne, Bay Rum, on my mug. A couple of shots of deodorant in strategic places and a fresh pair of skivvies were the next step. That one was followed by the final touch of a clean pair of khakis and a long sleeve cotton tee. I was reborn. I felt valuable to society again...until it was time to repeat the process of course.

Cleanliness and order are not matters of instinct; they are matters of education, and like most great things, you must cultivate a taste for them. -Benjamin Disraeli

"The Soulful Passage of Tommy Typical"

To a Tea

Ancient solution
The Chinese agree
Brown liquid potion
Is my cup to me

The story of tea is old by earth's standards. It began in China more than 5,000 years ago. Around campfires like the ones where I hung out as a kid, it has been said that Shen Nung, a wise emperor, who among other things required that all drinking water be boiled for health reasons. One day while on a trip he stopped to make camp. In accordance with his law, the servants began to boil water before they drank it. Some dried leaves from a bush fell into the boiling water, and a brown liquid formed. As a man who liked to try new things, the Emperor was interested in the novel brew. He drank some, and found it to be very good. And so, according to legend, tea was created. William Gladstone wrote, "If you are cold, tea will warm you. If you are too heated, it will cool you. If you are depressed, it will cheer you. If you are excited, it will calm you." Tommy says a glass of sweet tea in a large tumbler filled with ice cubes on a hot August afternoon while sitting in your favorite chair is as close to perfection as this earth life affords."

Sisters

She was the cheerleader with raven black hair,
Young Liz Taylor face and skin soft and fair,
"That's my older sister" I'd tell everyone,
She married one day and poof, she was gone.
Then came baby sister blonde & blue eyed
I carried her around boy full of pride
The years between us came into play
Eventually we had very little to say
Two sisters, two decades, two separate kinds,
They speak whatever they've got on their minds,
They've seen happiness and they've seen pain,
Cursed with a brother, wild and insane

You can kid the world. But not your sister.
Charlotte Gray

"The Soulful Passage of Tommy Typical"

Beech Grove

Half way between here and there
Is a stand of trees by a creek
Where thoughts are deeply probed
Barefoot scholars come near to seek
The pathway to newer paradigms
High roads to brave new places
Amid the past presently as future lies
Within brushwood loaded spaces

I see I hear I sense a feature
That I can not wholly explain
In Beech Grove I profess aloud
To be in silence is toward gain

Though a tree grows so high, the falling leaves return to the root.
-Malay proverb

Saint Francis of Bliss

In nature I found God's response
To questions my mind had sown
When I think I'm a little down
I find my garden fully grown
While counting fireflies a worthy task
Seeing art when a spider weaves
Discover that a soul at work
Knows what the heart believes
In performing simple tasks
One sees himself in all
Just being who he is
He heeds his Sweet Lord's call
St. Francis' voice resides
Within me as I aspire
The earth a sacred teacher
Indicates my soul's desire

It is no use walking anywhere to preach unless our walking is our preaching.
St. Francis of Assisi

"The Soulful Passage of Tommy Typical"

Lights out

Never know how much you miss it
Until the power goes out
Lighted candle becomes the norm
As you stumble all about

Electric world in the dark
Flashlight provides little sight
Shiver in the darkness
Mini universe without light

God is radiance the good book says
I trust that that is true
Because when blackout occurs
My faith comes into view

"Light always follows the path of the beautiful."
Unknown Second cousin of Tommy on his mother's side

Saintly Naps

You catch a few winks
And nod off for a while
It's so good to zzzzz
Wakefulness defile

A little relaxing jazz
A pillow and a throw
Then kick off the shoes
And there you go

You look like a an angel
When you're fast asleep
Wake up you baby cherub
From the heavy-eyed deep

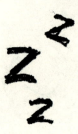

There is more refreshment and stimulation in a nap, even of the briefest, than in all the alcohol ever distilled. - Edward Lucas

I refresh and stimulate every chance I get. – Tommy Typical

"The Soulful Passage of Tommy Typical"

Mel the Builder

Why does a man from humblest beginnings
Carve out a life of momentous degrees
Seeking prosperity while fighting his battles
On an aircraft carrier in tropical seas;
From a hot noisy factory in California
'Cross motherland back to Tennessee
Where on a pastoral farm years before
He dreamt of what he might one day be;
America's promise for those who work
For those who will dare suppose
That real effort gives one the chance
As a consequence he slowly rose....
From a laboring man to selling goods
Erecting abodes his fortune found
Housing those with kindred dreams
A home on one's own ground

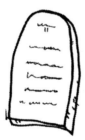

He didn't tell me how to live; he lived, and let me watch him do it. *Clarence Budington Kelland*

"He taught me that everyone needs a place they can call their home and their own." *Tommy on his father-in-law, Mel*

"In" Like Nanny

When we least expect her,
She appears at the door
And grabs us and hugs us,
Then sits on the floor,
And passes out fudge
Then hands over money,
After calling us names
Like Sweetie and Honey.
Her white hair is soft
She always smells sweet;
She kicks off her shoes
Walks around in bare feet;
You never quite know
What she'll say or she'll do;
When she'll come or she'll leave,
Ever smiling, never blue.
Her Good Book on the seat
Of her bright yellow truck;
With her overnight bag
She brings us all good luck;
When we visit her house
She cooks up a storm;
Tucks us in at night
Ensures we're safe and warm.
Some kids have grandmas
Rather solemn as a rule;
But I got my Nanny
And she's very cool!

My grandmother told stories; she was very good at that. *Cornelia Funke*

"The Soulful Passage of Tommy Typical"

Raise Your Voice

Dazed and confused. Happy.
Amused as we stumble into this world;
Joyful, I think. Bright lights make me blink!
...Let's try to make this work!
Are you going through ordinary life
Striving to achieve mediocrity?
When are we gonna realize that to see
you have to open your eyes and try?
Try pushing a little harder or going a little farther
If you want to change you voice your opinion,
Stand up and defend them.
Make an impact. Don't look back.
Do you think the great ones moved forward
by just standing around?
Simply giving up on their dreams
And just kept looking down
You can be up with your head in the sky
If you finally realize the power of "I"

My son, Jordan, wrote *Raise Your Voice* conveying what true soul is all about, namely self-realization. Now that makes a father proud. *Tommy being mentored by a fourteen year old*

My Way or the Hemingway

Images of Soul at Ten

Snow Angels and Sand Castles
Gnarly sticks as magic wands
Always made your best friends
Perform blood brother bonds
Wearing rubber band bracelets
Sip sweet honeysuckle treats
Swear on your granny's grave
To confirm your athletic feats
Seeking big daddy's "Attaboy!"
Mama's kiss so you won't weep
At bedtime raise a prayer to God
Your playful soul to keep

There are no seven wonders of the world in the eyes of a child.
There are seven million. -Walt Streightiff

If I only knew then how big *Little League* really was.
Tommy Typical on 1963

"The Soulful Passage of Tommy Typical"

A Dirge for Nadine
Celestial Journey of a Great Grandmother

For some 33,000 days our beloved Nadine resided with us as the sun rose and the sun set over the green hills of Middle Tennessee. Her supple skin was as fair and soft at ninety as any maiden of sixteen. Her ginger hair was sprinkled with wizened silver as it adorned her expressive face. The eyes sparkled like the surface of Old Hickory Lake just before twilight. Soft hands, tender yet knotted with age, had touched many wonderful things. Like princesses in fairy tales with consecrated hearts, she loved only one man and preferred to live in quiet solitude rather than quench the enchanting flame.

She toiled in her era and waked proudly among her peers impeccably adorned while bearing lovely daughters and amazing her friends with her wit and charm. A sharp and piercing sword has removed a piece of our souls with her passing and an empty divide exists in the depth of our spirits that connects us with our past. God seldom asks his children for what is already His by Divine and Holy right, but on a cold Christmas Day, He made a tender request for a gift that required a great sacrifice just like the gift He gave humankind. He took the delicate package and after unwrapping it carefully, gave it life anew and she was reborn as a pretty child that runs barefoot through fields of tall soft grass in a place where ten thousand days is a moment & young lovers hold hands eternally.

We are old and young at once, alive and dead at the same time.
Tommy Typical

Life's a Beach

Life's a canvas
...blank and ready to paint
...beautiful if you try
Life is breath
...draw in the ones you love the most
...watching the setting sun in the sky
Life is choice
...the things you desire to do
...the risks when you decide to take them
Life's the moment
...spent seconds in time
...wondering what you will make them
Life's a beach
Some days are surfing days
You ride on ocean blue
Some days are crazy days
A kid kicks sand on you

"When my daughter, Maddie whipped out this poem, I noticed not only her understanding of life, but her spontaneity and poignant expression. My children have filled my soul with beauty and understanding. I know yours have done the same for you. So we have a grave responsibility to bare our souls to them uncovered in the example of our lives well lived." *Tommy on daddy's eternal little girl.*

"The Soulful Passage of Tommy Typical"

Sardine Salad

I found a new seafood recipe
Buried deep in the L.A. Times
I substituted some lemon juice
I had no fresh squeezed limes

Added me some boiled taters
Some capers and white wine
Mixed in red onions and eggs
Served it up and it tasted fine

So read your newspaper everyday
The Sports page kindly do not waste
And while you peruse the financials
Don't forget the value of good taste

I will eat most anything that doesn't eat me first.
Tommy Typical on dietary restrictions

Mahalo

Thanks is all I can ever give
Thanks is all I'm able to say
Thanks for being truly alive
Thanks for another day

Thank You Lord for being God
Thank You for constructing me
And when I close my eyes
Being so thankful I <u>can</u> see

Gratitude is the flashing neon sign shaped
like a big arrow that points to a gracious soul.
Tommy Typical on spiritual and common courtesy

"The Soulful Passage of Tommy Typical"

May You Be in Divine Breath

I inhale and I exhale
And I pause in between
And I sense what I am
Beneath what can be seen
The clearest distinction
Between life and death
Is that gulp of fresh air
As you be in Divine breath

The soul of yours truly is in the end, as Elvis would sing, just a "hunk of burning love" and that's just fine because John the Elder wrote, "God is love, and he who abides in love abides in God, and God in him."
Tommy "Hickey" Typical on homecomings

Mele Kalikimaka

I put my verse ridden papers away and sat there in a land called *Hindsight*, remembering that nearby on July 1, 1961, after Ernest and Mary had dinner at the Christiana Restaurant, they simply went home. It's where we all end up. There early the next morning, Papa died from a self-inflicted gunshot wound and was buried in the Ketchum cemetery. When I first saw him at Sloppy Joe's I had a gut feeling that I was going to have the time of my life and I did. Now I needed some rest which I go. No dreams this time.

I got up early the next day and assumed that it was on a similar morning that Hemingway left here that time. I took a leisurely drive and ended up at Silver Creek about 45 minutes south of town. It is supposedly one of the best spring creek fisheries in the United States. The sluggish water is crystal clear and while I looked into it, Trout came to me for the last time on this leg of the holiday and I imagined he winked before he swam away. I looked at the evergreens that surrounded me and I thought about that one special Christmas morning that I try to keep recreating every holiday season. "Mele Kalikimaka!" St. Peter called out from across the way.

"Merry Christmas? I thought it was July," I said, though I wasn't really sure.

"It's always Christmas here. That's what you've been looking for, dreaming about, Isn't it Hickey?" Peter talked as he walked over to a clearing and produced a backpack that he handed to me. It was quite heavy, but reasonably manageable. He told me I might want to freshen up a bit as I smelled a little earthy. "Modesty wasn't necessary," he added, "no one would be coming by today."

So I removed my duds and climbed into the creek using the cold water to cleanse and refresh. After I got over the initial chilliness, I proceeded to wash myself and then to rinse my clothing. I pulled out a towel from the backpack and dried my body, then slipped into a pair of cotton chino pants, faded blue denim shirt, thick socks, and a pair of perfectly fitting hiking boots that "were just there". St. Peter had built a fire and I tied some rope between two trees and hung up the wet stuff to dry. He had boiled some water and made us each a cup of green tea which he served in tin cups sans lemon and sugar.

I told him I felt a little hungry and he reached into his backpack and handed me some thin white wafers and said they were manna. I remembered the story from the bible when the Israelites wandered in the desert and God rained down manna at night for his people to gather and eat the following day. They were coated with honey and were quite delicious. It was the best Christmas dinner I ever had.

An hour or so later, after my clothes dried and I repacked them, he handed me a split bamboo pole and a small leather bag with a fly reel and tackle. Everything was as light as a feather. Gravity was at bay. I held the rod for a second and it seemed to have been custom fit for my hand. It was perfectly balanced. I thanked him and put the bag in a sizeable outside pocket and inserted the rod in a slot on the side of the pack as Peter put out the fire and causally slipped on his pack. Everything seemed easy for him. It was getting easier by the moment for me.

He started out up the path lumbering along with a self-assured gait and I followed him. We were off. He started whistling first. After a while I started, too. I hadn't whistled in a while so I was a little rusty but it came back. We whistled the old standbys, and then did bird calls. Then I started it off and we whistled a medley of Broadway show tunes. And for a Grand Finale, I did a solo version of *Whistle While You Work.* Then we hummed for a spell and finally we sang. We took a break in the late afternoon each using a big oak tree as a backrest after dropping our backpacks. After a few minutes, I took a short siesta and dreamed about earth and when I awoke I saw him whittling on a soft hunk of wood.

"Where are we going? I asked as I chewed on a blade of grass I had pulled from the ground next to the tree trunk.

"Does it really matter? He answered.

"Not really. I was just curious."

"Let's walk up to that little rise. Our gear will be safe," he laughed. I *got* it and laughed, too.

St. Peter got up and stretched like a tom cat and then started walking. I strolled alongside and a few minutes later, we came to a clearing and from our elevated position I looked out over a big valley nestled between two jade ridges. The creek snaked its way right through the middle of the bottle green basin dotted with blossoming wild flowers. At the far end of the dale, there was a grouping of small cabins and one larger one that may have been a lodge. It was hard to tell as they looked like children's toys from this distance. I somehow knew the place was called Lakeside Resort.

"Are we going there?" I inquired.

"Yes, but we'll take our time. There's no rush at all. He's waiting for us there." He turned and headed toward our stuff. I lingered there for a few moments and took in the gorgeous vista. That place down there had a special charm to it even this far away. I had a hankering to get there.

When we stated walking again, out of the blue, St. Peter told me there were some cultures on earth that did not include the word *fiction* in their vocabulary. For them anything that you think has a basis in reality somewhere.

"Perhaps the thought is just waiting for the appropriate time to be revealed as something solid," I said.

"Perhaps," he replied, "you are learning a few things."

While I was considering that concept, he went on to say that Hemingway once wrote, "From things that have happened and from things as they exist and from all things that you know and all those you cannot know, you make something through your invention that is not a representation but a whole new thing truer than anything true and

"The Soulful Passage of Tommy Typical"

alive, and you make it alive, and if you make it well enough, you give it immortality. That is why you write and for no other reason that you know of. *But what about all the reasons that no one knows...Tommy Typical? Or what was it Papa called you? Hickey?*

"Yes," I answered.

"Do you remember the name you gave yourself, the one you loved as a kid?"

"Yes," I answered again, my memory juices percolating.

"What was it?" He inquired rhetorically.

"Koma." I replied remembering I had often imagined myself as a Hawaiian warrior living by the Blue Pacific and so I replaced my English name Tom for the exotic South Seas translation. I basked in those boyhood thoughts like my alter ego Koma must have basked in the Pacific sun.

St. Peter stirred me from my world of deliberation by touching me on the shoulder and saying, "And Koma, I will call you, but you will always be Tommy, too and Hemingway will forever remember you as Hickey. All one. All the same."

I pondered Papa's question and St. Peter's statement and was still lost in thought when he suggested we call it a day. Then I gathered some dry wood and we built another roaring fire by our rambling guide, the little trout stream that looked so much like the creek of my youth. We picked some blackberries from a nearby patch and he had some spicy beef jerky in his pack that he shared with me. We filled our tin cups with water and after noshing; we had another spot of tea and then bedded down around the warmth of the smoldering logs. I was beginning to understand where you go when you are gone.

As I was dozing off, which for dreamers is really waking up, a kind of darkness overtook the waning fire and in my soul, I heard St. Peter say, "*About all the reasons that no one knows,* old friend, Trust me. God knows."

Printed in the United States
52264LVS00002B/160-183